The *should have*

It must be some mistake, Joelle th
hideous mistake. Dancer wasn't dead.
be.

Joelle's father embraced her hard.
flop into his strong arms. *No. No. N*
horrible nightmare. Some late-night horr

But then she pulled away and l
weary faces of the two men. It was
her beloved horse, was dead!

"I hope the foal makes it," Dr. Butle

"The foal? You're worried about
foal that killed my Dancer? I don't c
pens to that stupid foal! I'll never forg

Tears blinding her, Joelle spun arc
away from the barn, away from the li
Dancer's stall, away from the awful
into the black night.

J PB
THOROUGHBRED

Don't miss these exciting books from HarperPaperbacks!

Collect all the books in the THOROUGHBRED series:

THOROUGHBRED Super Editions:

Ashleigh's Christmas Miracle

Ashleigh's Diary

Ashleigh's Hope

Samantha's Journey

ASHLEIGH'S THOROUGHBRED Collection:

Star of Shadowbrook Farm
by Joanna Campbell

The Forgotten Filly
by Karle Dickerson

Battlecry Forever
by Joanna Campbell

*coming soon

THE FORGOTTEN FILLY

KARLE DICKERSON

HarperPaperbacks
A Division of HarperCollins*Publishers*

▲ HarperPaperbacks

A Division of HarperCollins*Publishers*
10 East 53rd Street, New York, NY 10022-5299

Most HarperPaperbacks are available at special quantity discounts
for bulk purchases for sales promotions, premiums, or
fund-raising. For information, please write:
Special Markets Department, HarperCollins Publishers,
10 East 53rd Street, New York, NY 10022-5299

ISBN 0-06-106486-6

Cover illustration © 1993 by Daniel Weiss Associates, Inc.

First printing: January 1993
Reissue edition printing: July 1998

Printed in the United States of America

Visit HarperPaperbacks on the World Wide Web at
http://www.harpercollins.com

❖ 10 9 8 7 6 5 4 3 2 1

39464202

THE
FORGOTTEN
FILLY

One

TWELVE-YEAR-OLD JOELLE LATHAM LEANED UP AGAINST the white paddock fence with her back toward the black Thoroughbred mare within. Although Joelle could barely hear the horse's hooves as they padded through the soft grass, she knew the mare was approaching. Joelle smiled. Just a few more seconds. Let the mare think she was fooling her. Let her think this once she'd get close enough to nibble on Joelle's shoulder without being seen. Just a little closer . . .

"Boo! Gotcha!" Joelle suddenly spun around and looked her horse in the eye. Dance Away snorted and reeled back on her powerful hindquarters. She threw back her finely tapered head and flared her nostrils. Then she rocketed away at a gallop, letting her muscular legs carry her to the other end of the paddock.

1

"Hey, you sneaky horse, come back over here," Joelle said, slipping under the paddock fence and laughing. Dancer stood at the other end of the paddock and gave her a reproachful look.

"I'm sorry," Joelle said. "I guess you're not in the mood for any teasing today." She pulled a carrot out of her jeans pocket and held it up. Dancer's curved ears pricked up and she whickered softly. Then she ambled over to Joelle and gobbled down the treat. Joelle ran her hand over the distinctive white star on Dancer's nose, then rubbed her ears, letting her hand slide down the horse's glossy neck, tenderly smoothing aside her silky, cascading black mane. "I'd love to stay here all day and play with you, but I've got a ton of work to do," Joelle said. "It's Saturday, you know, and Saturdays get busy around here."

Joelle's eyes traveled over Dancer's broad back and down toward her full, round belly. Joelle couldn't resist pressing her ear up against it. Maybe she would at last hear the heartbeat of the foal. Instead she got a nudge in the side of her face.

"Hate to tell you, Mama, but you're going to have your hands full with this baby. She's going to be an active foal."

Dancer nickered softly, low in her throat, as if in agreement. Joelle lifted her head. From where she was standing, she could see the entire southern California town of Monte Vista laid out before her. Directly below, Joelle could see Windswept Riding Academy's barns, rings, and paddocks. She could

2

see where the new barn was being built, and she could hear the rhythmic pounding of hammers. It was almost nine o'clock and already her father and the construction crew had been out working on the framing of the new barn for three hours. Joelle's eyes scanned the skeleton of the barn, then moved on to the front road. A couple of cars were already turning in Windswept's gate. Joelle sighed. The day was starting. Just then, she saw a small figure in a neon-green wheelchair approaching the path that led up to the paddock.

"Hey, horse breath! Mom's looking for you! You're supposed to have the riding board ready by now. The lesson kids are gonna be here any minute."

Dancer snorted at the sound of Joelle's six-year-old brother's voice. Joelle watched as he drew closer and threw a soggy tennis ball for the barn dogs who were surrounding his chair. It had been only five months since Jeff had fallen out of a high tree he'd been climbing. He'd crushed several lumbar vertebrae, and had become partially paralyzed from the hips down. A few weeks later he'd undergone surgery to relieve pressure on the nerves in his spine and to regain the normal curvature of his spine. Then had come the wheelchair and the realization that the chances were good Jeff might never walk again. He'd had daily physical therapy sessions, but so far they hadn't done much for him. Jeff hated exercising almost as much as he hated being in a wheelchair, and Joelle knew he was uncooperative with his therapists.

As an older sister, Joelle had always felt protective of Jeff. After all, she'd been helping her mother take care of him ever since she was six. Since the accident, she'd spent more time with him than ever. Jeff shared her love of animals, and Joelle was always amazed at how he connected with every animal he met. They seemed drawn to him.

"I'm coming, cookie breath," Joelle called back. She turned to her mare and gave her a hug. "I wish the creek hadn't dried up; I bet you'd love to have your puffy legs soaked this afternoon. I'll see you later."

Joelle wiggled back under the paddock rail and was immediately engulfed by a mob of eager barn dogs. "Hey, Wolfie!" she said, patting the large, mangy dog that her father swore was half coyote. Then there was Whiskers, a gray Australian shepherd, and Carpy, a large yellow dog. Carpy planted her paws on Joelle's chest, sending them both backward into a heap in the dirt.

"Oh, you dogs!" Joelle said with mock annoyance.

She got up and dusted the powdery dirt off her jeans, then wiped the sweat from her forehead with her sleeve. It was hot. *If only this drought would end soon*, Joelle thought. There hadn't been much rain for two years, and for a while it hadn't mattered. All the sunny days had been good for the Latham family's riding-school business. Dry weather meant that horses could be worked every day in the large outdoor ring and that riding lessons were rarely canceled due to rain.

But the previous spring it had become clear that the drought meant more than just a low creek. Joelle had heard her parents talking late at night about rising water bills and mandatory water rationing. They'd begun cutting down drastically on water use. No more long hose baths for the horses in the wash racks—sponge baths only. And with the exception of the paddock grass, which was irrigated by hand with reclaimed water, all the grass on the Windswept grounds was turning brown.

"Have you been down to the new barn this morning?" Joelle asked her brother as she walked along beside his wheelchair.

Jeff smiled. "Yeah, but I got yelled at."

Joelle frowned and ruffled his hair. "What for, you troublemaker?"

"All I did was spin wheelies in the sawdust. One of the construction guys said I was in the way."

"Well, it won't be much longer until the barn's finished. And then we'll get some new school horses."

"New school horses? Why?" Jeff asked.

"Mom and Dad are hoping to attract some new students," Joelle told him. "That's why we've been going to more shows lately and putting up flyers everywhere. If we get more students, we'll need more school horses. And when we get more horses, that's where we're going to put them—in the new barn by the creek."

"Will Dancer and her foal be in the new barn, too?"

Joelle nodded and smiled. Dancer's foal would be born in only a few more weeks, and Joelle couldn't wait. It would be so exciting!

Joelle's father had been surprised when she'd brought up the subject of breeding her horse the winter before. "We're a riding school, not a breeding farm," he'd said.

Joelle had tried to explain. She knew how lucky she was to have a horse of her own—but someone else had trained her before the Lathams bought her for Joelle's eighth birthday. Joelle wanted a chance to raise and train a foal by herself. Maybe she could train the foal to be a champion.

The explanation had come out kind of jumbled. But it must have worked, because her father's tanned face had crinkled up in a smile, and he'd said, "It will be a lot of work, and we really don't have the facilities to handle a foal on this place. But if you want a foal out of Dancer that badly, we'll give it a try—even if it is a crazy idea. If there's one thing I understand, it's people who are horse-crazy—like me."

Joelle had jumped up and down and thrown her arms around her father like a little kid.

"Of course, you know foals are nonstop work," her father had said, growing serious once she'd calmed down. "And after Dancer's bred, she can't be worked as much. You won't be able to ride her after the big Oak Meadows fall show, and probably not for the entire year. And when the foal's born, you'll have to halter-break it and lead-break it. You'll have to trailer-break it and teach it to stand still for the farrier. And that's just the beginning. You of all people know that you can't even start riding the foal until it's at least two years old." He had looked straight into her eyes. "Are you prepared to take on all this responsibility?"

"Dad, you know I'll work hard," Joelle had replied.

Her father had nodded. "I know how hard you work around the place now. But a foal will require much more work. And another thing—there are no guarantees. You could pour your heart into this foal, but it might not be another Dance Away."

"There could be only one Dance Away," Joelle had declared loyally. But she knew that foal would be wonderful. After all, Dancer would be its mother!

Her father had called his trainer friends and found a stallion named Trilogy who'd won several international jumping competitions. Dancer had been bred at the end of April the previous year, and now it was early March—almost time for the foal to arrive. Just thinking about Dancer's foal made Joelle's heart feel light. She wanted to skip and sing and shout. Life was so good!

"Race you to the barn, Jeff," she said impulsively

as she broke into a run. The dogs barked and loped after her.

"No fair!" shouted Jeff, but he pushed the control on the side of his wheelchair and shot after her. She slowed, and in a short time he had caught up to her. "Cheater!"

Joelle let her brother pass, and he zipped into the barn ahead of her. Still breathing heavily from her sprint, Joelle followed him into the office. She waved her hands at the dogs, who weren't allowed inside. Her mother was at the desk, talking on the telephone.

Joelle waited while Mrs. Latham crossed a name off the list in her scheduling book and rewrote it under another time. Then she took the book from her mother and walked over to the board. Next to the trainers' names and times she carefully copied down the riders' names, which ring they were to use that morning, what time their lessons would take place, and which horse they would ride.

Joelle wondered why Bluebell's name wasn't on the list. The pony was the favorite of all the children and he never missed a Saturday. Mrs. Latham hung up the phone, but it rang again before Joelle could ask her about Bluebell.

"Good morning, Windswept Riding Academy. May I help you?" she said. "Oh, Gerald, it's you. I'm glad you're on your way. We have a couple of horses for you to look at today. Soldier's leg is stocked up, and I'd like you to check Bluebell's stitches. I'm afraid he's been at them."

Mrs. Latham finished her conversation with Gerald Butler, Windswept's veterinarian, and hung up the phone. "Whew," she said. "We've had a crazy morning—and no barn manager. Laura hurt her back when she was thrown from Ghost yesterday, so I have to cover for her. Plus one of the grooms packed up and left in the middle of the night. Joelle, where have you been? Classes will be starting soon."

"Sorry," Joelle replied. "I was having a talk with Dancer."

"You and that horse. Don't you two ever run out of things to talk about?" her mother asked with a laugh.

Joelle shook her head. "Nope. She's my best friend. Well, except for Nicole. But she doesn't count. She's a human. I mean, she does count. But Dancer is my best horse friend."

"I see," her mother said. She stood up and took one last sip from her coffee cup. Then she straightened some horse magazines on the coffee table in front of the desk. "When you're finished with the board, would you please clean up this office? We have to keep up our standards if we're going to compete with Oak Meadows Riding Club. We lost two students last week because the mothers wanted a nicer place to sit and chat while their daughters are riding. Can you imagine that? I thought people came to a riding school to learn how to ride, not to sit and relax." She glanced at her watch. "I have just enough time to run down to the new barn and see how your father is coming along before I start my first lesson. Do you want to come, Jeff?"

"Sure."

When they were gone, Joelle turned her attention back to the board and finished writing in the names. She had wanted to tell her mother not to worry about losing Melanie Hawkins and Darcy Jennings to Oak Meadows. They were snobs, perfect for Oak Meadows Riding Club! In Joelle's opinion, Windswept's office was a great place to hang around. Its paneled walls were covered with old photos of famous Windswept horses and riders, including her parents. Her father's Horseman of the Year award stood gleaming in a trophy case. Her mother had decorated with comfortable leather couches and horseshow-print armchairs. There were shelves lined with horse books propped up by dusty silver trophies. It was much nicer than Oak Meadows' stark, modern club room.

Still, Joelle's pride inspired her to straighten up the room. As she worked she caught a glimpse of herself in the horse-harness mirror that hung on the far wall. She stopped to study her reflection for a minute. Sandy blond hair that hung straight to her shoulders. She wished it had some curl to it. Nice enough blue eyes. A few freckles that she could do without. Joelle stepped back until she could see her entire image. At least she was tall and thin and had long legs.

Just then the screen door flew open, and Nicole Lattimer, Joelle's best friend next to Dancer, clomped into the room in her boots.

"Hey, Joelle," Nicole said breathlessly, tossing her thick black curls off her shoulders. Nicole always wore the wildest, brightest clothes. That day she was wearing jeans, a bright pink T-shirt, and pink high-tops to match. "Who am I riding today? I wish I had my own horse. You're so lucky—you have a whole stableful. Tell me that your mom didn't assign me Valor. He's been such a turkey, running away with me around the jump courses."

Joelle couldn't help laughing at how fast her friend jumped from one thought to the next. It was Nicole's never-ending sorrow that she couldn't have her own horse. But she didn't let that stop her. She rode any horse she could and was a gutsy rider. And most of Windswept's riders were envious that she got to ride Valor, a big bay with white stockings who was one of the best show horses they had. But lately she'd been having problems with the sensitive gelding. Joelle knew that it was due to Nicole's bold, aggressive style, but Mr. Latham hadn't been able to convince Nicole of that.

Joelle smiled. She knew Nicole would be pleased at her assignment. "You're riding Jupiter. I guess you're getting a break."

Nicole gave a huge sigh of relief. "Good. I'll go get her tacked up."

"Wait for me," Joelle said, trotting after her friend.

Nicole kept up a steady stream of talk as the girls entered the tack room and started gathering up their equipment. Joelle laid out several saddles on the saddle racks. Then she hung out bridles, double-checking that they all had the right bits attached.

When all the equipment for the morning's first lesson was in place, Joelle headed down the barn aisle to start bringing out the horses. She led Snicker to her spot in the crossties, then Chips and finally Jupiter. Within a short while, A Barn was filled with the noisy laughter and chatter of the students as they set about grooming their horses.

Joelle moved toward Bluebell's stall. She winced when she saw the place where he'd ripped open his stitches.

"You bad boy," Joelle scolded gently. She and Nicole had learned to ride on Bluebell, and though Dancer was first in Joelle's heart, she had a soft spot for the mischievous Welsh pony. "You were supposed to let that gash heal." She opened the stall door, slipped inside, and took a closer look at the pony's neck wound. A couple of days earlier Bluebell had somehow managed to pull his metal feed bin off the barn wall and cut his neck on a jagged edge. It had been healing nicely, and Bluebell would have been ready to work had he not ripped the stitches open. "Well, never mind. Dr. Butler is on his way, and he'll sew you back up."

Even as Joelle was saying this, she heard several shouts of "Hi, Dr. Butler" and "Hi, Devin." Joelle was annoyed that Dr. Butler's twelve-year-old son was with him. Devin was trouble. Joelle had known him all her life, and she'd thought he was nice enough when they were little. But a year earlier, his older sister had been killed in a drunk-driving accident, and he'd been acting like a jerk ever since. Joelle felt horrible about his sister, but Devin didn't have to act like such a creep because of it. He seemed determined to create problems whenever he could. She had heard he'd been kicked out of his last school; now he went to Fire Canyon Middle School with Joelle. He'd recently gotten a couple of nice horses and rode at Oak Meadows Riding Club. And he was always causing problems at horse shows. Once he had sprung out from behind some bushes on his horse, spooking the other riders' horses. The previous summer, he'd cut Joelle off at the ring rail during a class, causing her to lose her stride. He'd done things like that to other riders, too.

"Morning, Joelle," Dr. Butler called. He was a tall, thin man who seemed to be part horse himself as he strode gracefully down the concrete aisle. Joelle liked him a lot. It was too bad his son was such a pain.

"Hi," Joelle called back.

"What have we here?" Dr. Butler asked as he approached Bluebell's stall.

Joelle laughed at Bluebell's guilty expression. "He knows he's in trouble," she said as Dr. Butler set down his medicine case. Devin thrust out his

13

chin at Joelle in what she figured was some sort of greeting. She ignored him and slipped on the pony's halter. She held Bluebell as Dr. Butler cleaned the wound and got to work restitching it. Devin stood silently, almost sullenly, dispensing gauze, antiseptic powder, and scissors as his father needed them. Joelle couldn't figure out what his problem was. He was so different from his father. Dr. Butler was calm and easy around people and horses, and Devin . . .

"There we go," the veterinarian finally announced, patting Bluebell's dark gray shoulder. "Now, you stinker, leave this alone and let it heal."

"I don't think he's listening," Joelle said with a laugh. "He's already plotting how he's going to get at those stitches."

They all moved out of Bluebell's stall.

"How's that mare of yours, Joelle?" Dr. Butler asked.

"She's fine—I just left her sunbathing in the paddock on the hill."

"Good, good. Only a couple of weeks until her foal is due," Dr. Butler mused. "I saw Trilogy win another grand prix on TV last weekend. What a stallion! He's got great bloodlines. His dam, Fleet of Heart, was a spectacular jumper herself."

"She won several grand prix, didn't she?" Devin cut in, suddenly interested in the conversation. Joelle looked up in surprise. She hadn't realized that he knew much about horses. All he seemed to be interested in was causing trouble for people who hung around horses!

"Yes," Dr. Butler confirmed. "Dancer certainly married herself up with a great jumper of a stallion."

Joelle beamed. She and Dr. Butler continued their conversation about Dancer as they made their way to her paddock. Partway up the hill, Joelle noticed that Devin had turned around and was watching Mrs. Latham's lesson in ring one. Joelle narrowed her eyes. Was he watching Nicole on Jupiter? He'd better not be planning any more pranks.

When they reached the paddock, Joelle whistled for her horse. Dancer lifted her lovely head and quickly approached. Joelle held the horse as Dr. Butler took out his stethoscope and listened first to Dancer's heartbeat, then to that of the foal, and checked her over thoroughly.

"Everything seems fine, but I like to keep an eye on older maiden mares who foal," Dr. Butler said as he put away his stethoscope.

Joelle was quick to jump on the uncertainty in his voice. "Why's that?" she asked.

"It's nothing to worry about. It's just that older mares sometimes have more complicated deliveries. But Dancer's been going through this pregnancy without any hitches. She's going to be fine."

As Joelle walked down the hill with Dr. Butler she tried to ignore the little bubble of worry that was forming in her stomach. But she looked at the vet's lined face and relaxed. He didn't seem to be worried.

15

"Thanks for looking at Dancer. I've got to get back and help out," she said. She waved to Dr. Butler as he walked away to continue his rounds.

The rest of the day was a whirlwind of activity. It seemed to Joelle that she never had time to take a breath. Horses to tack up, horses to cool off. Riders to manage. A zillion saddles to clean.

Finally, after supper, she slipped up to the paddock to lead Dancer down the hill to her warm, cozy stall. She paused on the path that led to the barn. The sun was setting, casting a brilliant pink glow across the mountains. The Santa Ana winds were kicking up, and Joelle watched as Dancer's glossy mane rippled in the hot breeze.

"Well, I've got a history project to get started on," she said. Dancer whuffled in her ear. "I wish I could spend more time with you," Joelle said, "but there's always so much to do around here. But soon you're going to foal and we'll be busy raising and training your baby. It'll be so exciting!"

Joelle let Dancer into her stall, gave her one final hug, and headed toward her house. It wasn't until that night, as she lay in the stillness of her dark room, that Dr. Butler's voice floated back into her mind. "I like to keep an eye on older maiden mares who foal."

Joelle shivered. Maybe she'd been wrong to breed Dancer. If anything ever happened to her horse, she knew she'd never forgive herself!

16

Two

"OWW! I DON'T WANT TO DO THESE STUPID EXERCISES!"

Joelle heard Jeff's howls all the way in her bedroom on Monday morning. She pulled her pillow over her head and groaned. The fact that Jeff was doing his exercises already meant that she was late getting up. Normally by this time, Joelle would have eaten and been down at the barn, saying good morning to Dancer. That way, she wouldn't have to listen to the tears and tantrums that were always part of Jeff's morning sessions with the therapist who came to the house.

Joelle sighed and threw back her covers. After her shower, she joined her father downstairs for breakfast. She could hear her mother helping Jeff take a bath.

"Another bad session?" she said glumly to her father.

"Yeah." Mr. Latham's face was tight. "Jeffrey's got to start working on his therapy program or he'll never make progress. It might be uncomfortable and boring, but I know he could get himself out of that wheelchair if only he'd work at it."

"You really think he could walk again?" Joelle asked hopefully, as if she hadn't asked the question a zillion times in the past few months.

Mr. Latham shrugged. "I've got to believe it. We can't give up believing it."

Joelle poured herself a bowl of cereal and waited for her mother and brother to put in their appearance.

A short while later Mrs. Latham came into the kitchen carrying a scowling Jeffrey. He was freshly bathed, his dark blond hair plastered to his head. Joelle could tell he'd been crying.

"Jeff, my man," Mr. Latham said, slapping him a high five. Jeff managed a lopsided grin, but he still wasn't happy.

"Hey, cookie breath, you okay?" Joelle said, passing the cereal to her brother.

"Therapy stinks," Jeff said sullenly. He poured his cereal, then started trying to do the maze on the back of the box.

Her parents turned their conversation to the day's scheduling while Joelle quickly ate her breakfast. With Dancer getting so close to foaling, she wanted to be sure to squeeze in a few minutes with her before she left for school. When she'd downed the last of her cereal, she dashed out to the barn.

18

"Good morning, everybody," Joelle sang out as she walked up the barn aisle. As usual, she had to wade through the eager barn dogs, who were waiting for their good-morning pats.

A few whinnies answered her, but mostly what she heard was the sound of munching. The stable hands had tossed hay in the racks an hour earlier and had fed the horses who needed their special supplements. Joelle waved to Laura, the barn manager, who was removing Soldier's leg wraps.

"How's your back?" Joelle asked.

"Fine. My own dumb fault. Not Ghost's," she answered, closely studying Soldier's leg. Then she straightened up painfully and patted the horse. "You're hardly stocked up at all. Looking better every day. I knew that my magic herbal remedy would do the trick."

Joelle smiled. Like Dr. Butler, Laura seemed to be part horse. Joelle was sure she even preferred their company to that of people. Wiry and tall, with long brown hair she wore in a ponytail, Laura even moved like a horse.

Joelle continued down the aisle to where Dancer's brass nameplate hung. She used her jacket sleeve to wipe away a smudge, and the words *Dance Away* gleamed brightly back at her. Dancer stood expectantly in the shavings-filled stall chewing on a mouthful of alfalfa.

"Hi, Mama," Joelle said, unlatching the stall door and sliding it open. Dancer nickered and ambled over to nuzzle Joelle's jacket.

19

"Good. You ate all your breakfast," Joelle said, rubbing her mare's white star. Her hands went into their familiar ritual: first the star, then the ears, over the neck, down the long, flowing mane, and finally to the belly. "Hi, foal. Whatcha doing in there? When do you plan to put in your appearance, anyway?"

Dancer nickered and tossed her elegant head.

"I know, Dancer. You're impatient, too. You want to meet this baby as much as I do," Joelle said.

Dancer nuzzled her, searching Joelle's pockets for carrots. "Forgot. Sorry. Anyway, I'm dressed for school, so if you wouldn't mind, I'd appreciate it if you wouldn't get any hay juice on my clothes."

She stroked Dancer's nose and neck until her father's voice boomed through the barn.

"Joelle Latham, get a move on. The school bus will be here any minute."

Joelle sighed and gave Dancer one last ear rub. "Coming, Dad," she called. "Now you behave yourself while I'm at school. Don't have that foal till I get home, okay?"

She hastily removed Dancer's blanket, stepped outside the stall, and hung the blanket on the rack. She looked up to see her father leading Great Caesar's Ghost, the big gray jumper, down the aisle. Joelle's heart swelled with pride at the sight of her handsome father in his riding clothes. He always believed in setting an example for his students. Hardly a lesson went by that he didn't drill them on the importance of dressing appropriately for the sport. And to set an example, Mr. Latham turned out for every lesson in impeccable riding clothes, his tall black boots gleaming with polish.

He'd pulled the gelding from his stall and was now heading to the crossties to groom him, the sound of his boot heels on the concrete floor ringing through the barn aisle.

"I wish I could stay here instead of going to school," Joelle said enviously as she stood on her tiptoes to plant a kiss on her father's cheek. "Sometimes I think school was invented just to take time away from horses."

Mr. Latham switched his riding crop and the reins to the other hand, then patted her on the shoulder. "I know how you feel. I used to think the same thing. But you know what?" Mr. Latham's blue eyes twinkled as he looked at his daughter. "I discovered something."

Joelle knew she was walking into one of her father's famous lecture traps. "What?"

"I discovered that there are a lot of lessons you can learn at school that apply to horses. Like self-discipline. Like working hard so that you can bring out the best in yourself. How can you bring out the best in your horse if you can't bring out the best in yourself? Well, anyway, scoot. You'll miss the bus. Your mother has already taken Jeff to school. She's going to talk with the therapist today. We've got to figure out a way to get Jeff interested in working on his program."

Just then Joelle heard the sound of the school bus horn.

"Bye, Dad. Have a good ride," she called, and bolted to the house to grab her backpack.

A few minutes later she was seated on the school bus, rattling her way toward Fire Canyon Middle School, wondering what was going to happen to Jeff. They weren't going to send him away or something, were they? The thought was too awful to bear. She forced it out of her mind.

Two stops later she was joined by Nicole, and a few minutes after that by Kendra Kenagy. Kendra had taken ballet for years, and had recently started riding at Windswept. She was naturally graceful in the saddle, and had classical form. Joelle thought she'd be a pretty good rider if she were a little less timid with the horses. Kendra slid into the seat across the aisle from Nicole and Joelle.

"Did you guys do your history outline? I can't believe our reports are due in two weeks," she said as soon as she was seated.

"Ugh. Mrs. Rubins is gonna give me the hardest time when she sees my outline," Joelle wailed as the bus rumbled off again. "I was so busy this weekend with the riding school, I hardly had time to work on it."

"I'm not that thrilled with mine, either," Nicole admitted ruefully. "There are so many things I'd rather be doing besides history."

"Me, too," Kendra chimed in.

"Like riding!" the three girls said in unison, and burst out laughing. "And speaking of riding, do you realize it's only two more weeks until the Oak Meadows spring horse show?" Nicole asked.

"Like I could forget," Joelle said. She didn't mention it, but the one thing that did disappoint her about breeding Dancer was that she couldn't ride her in this show. She'd dreamed about winning the Oak Meadows Riding Club spring championship trophy on Dancer for years now. And the year before, she'd ended up as reserve champion. The beautiful tricolor ribbon was one of her most prized possessions. She was sure that if Dancer hadn't been in foal this year, she and her horse would be the ones taking home the gleaming silver cup.

"We just have to beat Oak Meadows," Nicole said. "But they're so good."

"Well, they have some nice horses. But Windswept's horses are every bit as good," Joelle said. "And our riders have more heart. Nicole, if you could just settle down and not muscle Valor around the course so much, I think you'd have a good chance at taking the championship."

Nicole grinned and flipped back her dark hair nervously, setting her large hoop earrings dancing. "If only. Joelle, you make it sound so easy. I mean, I try. But sometimes I just start to get wigged out when I see all those jumps. I get so excited, I just want to get the course over with *now!*"

"It's great to be gutsy. But you still have to learn

to control your impulse to speed up if you want to show at higher levels," Joelle said firmly. "You can't race around a course and expect to have a smooth ride."

"I know, I know," Nicole wailed.

Kendra shook her head at Joelle's intensity. "You sound like your mom and dad. I'd like Windswept to win and all, but you know and I know we'd have a better chance if Devin Butler weren't around to distract us."

"Yeah, he makes me nervous," Nicole said, giggling.

Joelle snorted. "I don't know what it is about you guys and Devin."

Nicole shrugged. "Well, anyway, he'll be competing for Oak Meadows, and you have to admit he's a good rider. He'll make it harder for us to win."

Joelle nodded. "He's an okay rider, but he could stand some more work on the flat. Do you see the way he hunches forward? You have much better form when you put your mind to it."

"I like his form just fine," Nicole said under her breath.

"Me, too," Kendra added.

"It's not that good!" Joelle protested.

Kendra and Nicole both looked at their friend. "You really are horse-crazy!" Nicole said. "We weren't talking about his riding, in case you hadn't noticed."

Joelle straightened her long blue sweater and

rolled her eyes. "If you guys go boy-crazy on me, I'll never forgive you."

"Don't worry," Kendra said loyally. "Devin's cute, but we'd never abandon horses for him. And we're still interested in hearing about Dancer. How was she this morning? Does she look like she's going to foal soon?"

Joelle remembered Dr. Butler's comment about older mares foaling, but she forced that thought down. "Not for a couple of weeks, probably. Dr. Butler told me not to get too anxious, though he says a mare who hasn't given birth before is more likely to be late than early, and that it's impossible to pinpoint a date."

"Aren't you just dying to know what the foal will be like?" Nicole asked.

Joelle nodded, and her sandy blond bangs flopped forward over her eyes. Brushing them back, she caught a glimpse of her ragged fingernails and held them out for her friends' inspection. "See? I get so worked up waiting, I bite my nails and they look awful. I can't stand the suspense. And I'm dying to ride Dancer again. Do you realize it's been months since I've been on her back?"

"Well, you have an entire stable to pick from, so at least you can ride other horses," Kendra said.

"Yeah, but not one of them is Dancer."

When the bus dropped them off at school, the girls headed toward their lockers. At the sound of the warning bell they said good-bye and went their separate ways to class.

*   *   *

The day wasn't a total waste, Joelle told herself as she stepped on the bus to go back home after school. Mrs. Rubins hadn't been pleased at Joelle's lack of progress on her history project. But at lunchtime Joelle had managed to get over to the library and find a new book, *Your Foal's First Year.* If the bus hadn't been so noisy and crowded, she would have buried her nose in it right then. But instead she laughed and chatted with her friends some more about the upcoming Oak Meadows horse show.

The bus let a group of lesson kids off at the end of Windswept's driveway. Most of the kids headed straight down to A Barn to change and start their lessons, but Nicole and Joelle made their way up to the house. After grabbing a snack, they bounded upstairs to Joelle's room and tossed their backpacks on her bed.

"You've got the greatest room," Nicole said, looking around as she changed out of her jeans into her schooling sweats. She bunched up her jeans, stuffed them into her backpack, and pulled on her shirt.

"Thanks," Joelle said. Joelle liked her room, too. It was airy and comfortable, with horse posters covering the walls. Dancer's bridle hung over the back of her chair, waiting for the day when she could be ridden again. Model horses lined her windowsills and ribbons hung from the lamp by her bed. Framed pictures of herself and Dancer were everywhere. Her first saddle, now too small for her, had its own place of honor on a saddle rack in the corner. Some of her friends had more stylish rooms with fancy wallpaper and state-of-the-art stereos and TVs, but Joelle was sure there wasn't a more comfortable room in all of southern California.

Once dressed, the girls went down to the kitchen, grabbed their boots by the back door, and slipped them on as soon as they were outside. Then they walked down to A barn, where the other students were tacking up their horses in the crossties.

"Hey, doesn't the parking lot seem more crowded than usual?" Nicole asked as they headed toward the office to check the riding board for their assignments.

Joelle turned to look. "Yeah. Maybe we're getting some new students. You know, my parents are hoping to expand a little. That's why they're building the new barn." Joelle had helped them put up flyers at the grocery store announcing the spring lessons and knew they'd been running ads in the local papers as well.

When Joelle and Nicole entered the office, Mr. Latham was seated at the desk, talking to the mother of a girl Joelle recognized from school.

Her father looked up. "This is my daughter, Joelle. She's ridden practically all her life and she helps me run some of the classes. This is Tara McDaniels. She's going to start riding at Windswept."

The redheaded girl smiled shyly at Joelle. Joelle

smiled back and said hello. Then she and Nicole excused themselves, checked the riding board, and went out to tack up their mounts. Joelle was scheduled to ride Valor. Nicole had Jupiter again.

"Whew," Nicole said.

"Don't you like Valor anymore?" Joelle asked.

Nicole nodded. "Yeah. But I just hate to look like a fool on him. Maybe after another lesson on Jupiter, I'll be ready to tackle my problems on Valor again."

Joelle saddled and bridled Valor and led him down the aisle. She had Nicole hold the horse while she ducked into the tack room and grabbed both of their green schooling helmets. Then the girls walked out toward ring one. Joelle led Valor up to the mounting block outside the ring. Swinging her leg lightly over the cantle, she settled in gently on Valor's broad back. Then she leaned over to adjust the girth and slipped her feet into her stirrups while Nicole climbed aboard Jupiter.

Joelle noticed the group was fairly small as she entered the ring and started her warmup walk. Good. Sometimes Valor got excited and nervous in a big group of horses. He'd be more settled in a smaller group. She gave the horse a long rein, and let him drop his head.

"Hey, check it out, Joelle," Nicole said in Joelle's ear as she pulled up alongside her on Jupiter. She motioned with her chin over to ring two. Joelle's eyes followed Nicole's gaze. The next minute, she almost fell out of her saddle!

"It's—it's Jeff!" she said in amazement. "He's riding Bluebell!" Her mother was standing at Bluebell's head, her hands firmly on the lead rope. Jeff, in a dark helmet, was on Bluebell's back, with Laura holding his leg on one side. An older woman whom Joelle didn't recognize was standing next to Jeff's leg on the other side. Joelle turned and saw Mr. Latham entering the ring on Chips. She nudged Valor with her heels and urged him to walk toward her father. They met up at the ring gate.

"Dad, what's going on?" she burst out, pointing at Jeff with her riding crop.

Her father's face broke out in a delighted grin. "Mom's been checking this out for a while. She talked with Jeff's doctors, and they recommended a riding center where they teach disabled kids to ride. One of the volunteers—her name's Karen—agreed to come over today and show us how to work with Jeff."

Joelle couldn't believe it. Jeff was confined to a wheelchair. He had suffered a major spinal injury and had practically no feeling from his hips downward. How could he possibly ride?

"Dr. Holman says it could be good therapy for him," Mr. Latham went on. "Jeff's got good upper-body control. We found a deep dressage saddle that can support his back. He'll need lots of help at first, but riding just might help him gain confidence."

"But Dad, what if—what if Bluebell spooks or something?"

"Old Bluebell's steady and reliable with a rider

on his back, honey. Don't worry so much. You know we wouldn't be trying it if we didn't feel it was safe. We've been talking about it for a while, and we finally got the go-ahead today. Jeff was ecstatic, and nothing could stop him from trying."

"Why didn't you tell me?" she asked.

"I wanted to be certain it was a sure thing before I mentioned it. This family doesn't need any more disappointments. Now let's get started," he called in a louder voice. "We have work to do. At the sitting trot, please."

Nicole and Joelle turned their attention from Jeff and focused back on urging their horses into a balanced sitting trot. It was all Joelle could do to concentrate on her lesson. She kept looking over to the other ring to check on her little brother. Sure, there might be someone holding the pony and two people supporting Jeff, but her little brother wasn't in his wheelchair! He was sitting straight and tall, his fingers woven into Bluebell's bushy mane. Jeff was riding! After a few times around the ring, Mrs. Latham finally stopped Bluebell and lifted Jeff off the pony's back. Jeff held up his arms in triumph. "I did it!" he shouted.

At dinner that night, Jeff's cheeks glowed bright pink and his eyes sparkled. It reminded Joelle of the way he'd looked before his accident—all smiles, and a bundle of energy.

"I still can't believe you were riding," Joelle said, offering Jeff the mashed potatoes.

"Yeah, I know. It was great. But just wait. Next time I'm going to canter," he bragged.

"Slow down, son," Mr. Latham said. "We just got started."

"We'll work up to cantering a little bit at a time," Mrs. Latham added. "For now we'll start at a walk and see how you do."

"Walking's too slow," Jeff protested. "I want to go faster."

Joelle said, "You were great. You looked like you'd been riding Bluebell forever. You'll be cantering before you know it."

Jeff sat up straighter and served himself a gargantuan pile of potatoes. "Soon I'll be riding just like my horse-breath sister."

After she'd cleared the table and loaded the dishwasher, Joelle went up to her bedroom to start her homework. Chewing on the end of her pencil, she alternated between working on her history outline and staring out at the night sky. So much was going on. Between thinking about Jeff's riding and Dancer's foal, she could barely concentrate on her schoolwork. She was sure the foaling would go smoothly for Dancer. After all, things were looking up for the Latham family.

Three

"MAIL'S HERE! I HEAR THE TRUCK," JOELLE CALLED AT lunchtime on Saturday. She stood up from the table. "Let's see if we got the premiums today for Oak Meadows."

"I'm coming, too," Jeff said. He followed Joelle out the door in his chair. "I had Mom order me a new cartridge for my video game. It's just got to come today."

When they reached the mailbox, they sorted quickly through the pile of mail.

"It's here!" Jeff grabbed a package and started opening it.

Joelle flipped through the stack until she saw the familiar Oak Meadows logo. "We got the show premium, too."

Just then a group of boys rode by on their bikes. They were laughing and challenging each other to a race. Jeff looked up from his game and watched them whiz by. He set the game in his lap and wheeled furiously back to the house.

"Jeff, wait for me," Joelle called, trotting after him. She hated when something like this happened. She knew how awful Jeff felt about not being able to do the things most kids could.

"I hate those kids," Jeff gasped as he wheeled up the ramp to the house.

"Jeff, you can ride a horse. And that's a lot harder than riding a silly old bike. I'd like to see those boys try to ride your pony," Joelle said.

Jeff's eyes searched her face, but then he entered the house abruptly.

Once inside, Joelle told her mother what had happened and they both tried to coax Jeff out of his bad mood, but he turned on his video game and refused to talk.

Joelle sighed and went down to the barn to see Dancer.

"Look at this prize list, Dancer," Joelle said, brandishing the yellow piece of paper.

The mare blew puffs of air into Joelle's ear and tossed her head up and down a couple of times. Joelle stroked her absently while scanning the list. Then she looked up at her mare. "I know. You wish we could go and win a few ribbons, but we can't. Your figure isn't what it used to be." Joelle chuckled softly at her joke. "Never mind. You'll have it back soon. And we'll go next year."

Joelle looked at the list again. If she *could* ride

Dancer in this show, she'd take her in the hunter classes and the medal classes and . . . Joelle's thoughts trailed away from her horse-show fantasy. Maybe she'd been wrong to breed Dancer. She missed showing her, and her father had been right—managing a brood mare had been a lot of work and worry so far. And the foal wasn't even born yet.

"Hurry up and have your foal, Dancer. I can't wait to start riding you again. Just think of all the ribbons we'll win next spring," Joelle murmured as she led Dancer out to her paddock on the hill. She unfastened the halter and watched as the horse ambled away and began grazing.

"See you later," Joelle called, turning back to A Barn.

As she approached the crosstie area, Joelle saw that her mother and Jeff were grooming Bluebell. Karen, the volunteer who had helped Jeff the other day, was there, too.

"Going for a ride?" she asked her little brother.

"Uh-huh." Jeff flashed her a big smile as he leaned over to brush Bluebell's flanks.

"Hi, guys." Joelle turned to see Nicole entering the barn. She carried a bag of carrots and a bag of apples. "I got here early so that I could bribe Valor with some treats before my lesson."

"Karen, this is Nicole, Joelle's friend," Mrs. Latham said. "Karen's a volunteer with Forward With Horses. It's a center for therapeutic riding."

Karen nodded hello, then continued helping Jeff

get ready for his lesson. Nicole watched as Mrs. Latham removed the saddle cover from a gleaming new saddle.

"Wow, that's gorgeous," Nicole breathed, running her hand over the soft leather.

"We drove down to the tack shop today and picked this up. The dressage saddle we were using wasn't quite right. We had this one specially fitted," Mrs. Latham explained. She took it off the saddle rack and held it up for the girls' inspection.

"It looks like a dressage saddle, only lighter," Joelle commented, lifting the flaps and running her hands over the smooth seat with its high cantle.

"It's extra-close contact—there's not as much padding under the leather—so Jeff can really feel the horse's movements through his legs. The warmth stimulates his muscles."

Mrs. Latham put on Bluebell's saddle and then his bridle. Joelle pushed Jeff's wheelchair outside to the mounting block while her mother led the pony.

"Look at the stirrups. They're breakaway stirrups. They have a thick rubber band instead of the usual iron for safety," Karen explained.

Joelle let out a low whistle as she examined the special stirrups. "You're all ready to ride," she said to Jeff.

"After he puts on his riding helmet," Mrs. Latham reminded him.

Joelle watched her mother and the therapist gently settle Jeff on the pony's back. Karen immediately took up a post at Jeff's side, supporting his back with one hand, while tightening his pants leg and clamping his leg next to the saddle with the other hand. Laura walked over and took her place on the other side.

"What are they doing?" Nicole asked.

"They're the sidewalkers," Joelle explained. "They help keep Jeff secure in the saddle. Well, time for you to get ready for your lesson," she said to Nicole. "Here comes Kendra."

Joelle stopped to talk with Kendra for a minute, then she wandered through the barn and up to Dancer's paddock to watch her graze. A little while later, she put Dancer back in her stall and went to the tack room. As she approached she could hear laughter and talking.

"What's going on here? A tack-cleaning party?" she asked, stepping inside.

Nicole was sitting on a bench, lathering up a saddle with a sponge. Kendra was running another soapy sponge down a length of rein hanging from a tack hook. Several other kids were busily soaping and polishing equipment. Jeff was leaning over the side of his wheelchair, dipping several grimy snaffle bits into a bucket of water.

"Your dad," Kendra said simply.

Joelle didn't need any further explanation. She could imagine her father walking into the tack room to grab his equipment and noticing the dirty condition of even one piece of leather. The next minute, he'd have commandeered every rider on

Windswept's grounds and set them to work cleaning every piece of equipment in the tack room. "There's a horse show in only a week. Look at this mess!" he'd say indignantly.

"He wasn't happy," Nicole added, rubbing her sponge along a glistening bar of glycerine saddle soap.

"I told my mom she'd have to wait for me even though my riding lesson was over. Mr. Latham told me I had to clean a saddle before I could leave," said a girl Joelle didn't recognize. She was sitting on the bench by Nicole. "I don't mind, but my mom doesn't like horses."

Joelle knew she must be one of the new riders who had just registered for lessons. "I'm Joelle. Mr. Latham's my father. I can finish your saddle if you have to go," she offered.

"No thanks. I kind of like doing it. I've got Snicker's saddle, and she's a great horse."

"Don't use too much water or my dad will give you a big lecture," Jeff piped up, watching her dip her sponge into the water bucket. He dried the bits he was cleaning and started wiping off some others.

"'Using too much water is one of the surest ways to ruin good leather that I know of,'" Nicole mim-icked Mr. Latham's gruff lecturing voice.

Joelle smiled at her friend's imitation. "Sometimes my father is so strict," she said. She lifted Soldier's saddle off its rack and sat on the bench next to Nicole.

"No one's complaining," Kendra told her. "Your parents are the best trainers around. They're much better than the trainers at Oak Meadows."

"I used to ride at Oak Meadows," said the new girl. "And actually, the trainers weren't all that bad."

All eyes in the tack room turned to look at her, but she just shrugged. "It was nice there. The place is beautiful, and they have a big-screen TV in the club room. But . . ." She paused. "Actually, they care more about how expensive your horse is and how expensive your riding clothes are. I like Windswept. You guys care about the horses."

Joelle's heart glowed with pride. "Thanks. That means a lot to me and my folks."

"At Oak Meadows we had grooms to get the horses ready and clean the equipment. All we had to do was ride. I've only had a few lessons at Windswept, and I've already learned how to tack up and how to clean a saddle. It makes me feel more in charge knowing how to do things by myself."

"That's the way my parents feel," Joelle said, pulling the stirrup leathers off the saddle and sliding off the irons. "But we never underestimate Oak Meadows. They have good riders, and we're going to have to watch out for them at this horse show. Only a week to go."

"We'll win the championship," Kendra said loyally, looking over at Nicole. "I just know it."

Nicole looked uneasy. "I hope so. I didn't have the greatest lesson today. The bribes didn't work.

Valor still tore around the course. Jeez, Joelle, I wish you could ride Dancer this year. You'd win for sure and take the heat off me."

"Joelle, why can't you ride some other horse in the show?" Jeff asked. "You like Soldier."

Joelle rubbed her sponge along the glycerine bar. She closed her eyes and tried to picture herself riding some other horse at a show. She couldn't do it. "I haven't ridden at a horse show on anyone but Dancer since I got her. I just don't think I could show any other horse. I can school other horses, but I don't want to show them."

"You can't show any other horse but Dancer? That's dumb—Dancer's not the only horse in the world," Jeff said, stopping his bit cleaning to look at his sister. His smudged face plainly showed his disapproval.

"You wouldn't understand, Jeff," Joelle said softly. "To me, she's the only horse in the world."

"But won't you ride her foal in shows when it gets bigger?" he persisted.

"Jeff, you're a pest," Joelle exclaimed. The foal wasn't even born yet, and people were already making plans for it. Not that she hadn't imagined Dancer's foal winning ribbons. But now that the foal's birth was imminent, Joelle was beginning to think it was bad luck to talk about what it would be like when it grew up. Ever since Dr. Butler had hinted that Dancer might have a complicated delivery, Joelle hadn't stopped worrying. And even if everything went all right with the delivery, the foal might not turn out to be that special.

"Horses are a gamble. You breed them, you take your chances." Joelle could hear her father's voice as clearly as if he were in the room.

On Sunday evening, Joelle flopped on her bed and plodded her way through her homework. She forced herself to keep her mind on her work, and finally managed to finish the dreaded history outline. Then she started her science homework. Why couldn't Mr. Whiting assign more interesting stuff than a chapter on the microscopic animals that lived in pond water? Why couldn't they study something like the stages of development of a foal? Joelle propped her elbows on her desk and tried to picture Dancer's foal forming inside her.

After she'd changed into her pajamas and brushed her teeth, Joelle slipped into bed with her new horse book. Instantly, her eyes were drawn to the pictures of the foaling mare and the birth.

Joelle's eyes scanned the pages until her mother called up that it was time for her to turn out her light. "You need your beauty sleep," her father chimed in as he came in to kiss her good night.

Joelle flipped out her light, but when she heard her father go downstairs, she turned on her flashlight under the covers so she could continue reading. How could she sleep? The birth of a foal was too exciting!

The week flew by, and on the following Sunday,

the morning of the horse show, Joelle woke up before dawn. But still she had a sense that she was late, and tore off her covers to make a beeline for the bathroom and a hot shower. After she'd toweled off, she pulled on the clothes that she'd laid out the night before. Even though she wasn't riding in the show, she would be representing Windswept. She put on her best breeches, her white ratcatcher blouse, and her lucky choker pin. You could never tell when you'd need an extra bit of luck at a horse show.

Horse shows were important to her family. The kids who rode in them liked the experience, but they also liked to win ribbons and trophies. And their parents, who paid for the riding lessons, were pleased when their kids were rewarded for their hard work. When the Windswept students did well at the shows, it reflected well on the riding school and the hard work of Joelle's family.

Joelle brushed her wet hair into a ponytail and tied a blue ribbon around it. Then she hurried down to the kitchen in her stocking feet. Her mother was already up, making coffee and preparing sandwiches. Joelle made herself a bowl of oatmeal.

"Is Dad up yet?" she asked, sitting down at the table with her breakfast.

"He's been up for hours already," her mother said. "One of the braiders didn't show up, so he's been helping Laura with the braiding. I just took his breakfast down to the barn." Joelle shot her a questioning look. "Dancer's fine, dear. Waiting for her feed, just like any other morning."

Joelle let out a sigh of relief and continued attacking her oatmeal. A moment later, she heard a rustling in the room next door. Once it had been the family room, but after the accident it had been converted into a bedroom for Jeff. Soon her brother's sleepy head appeared around the door, and he wheeled himself into the kitchen.

"What's everyone doing up so early?" he mumbled. His hair was sticking up all over the place and his pajamas were rumpled.

"Morning, sleepyhead," Mrs. Latham said, giving him a kiss and a squeeze. "It's horse-show day, remember? Joelle and Dad have to shove off early."

Jeff looked blearily at Joelle. "Oh, yeah. Can I go?" he asked.

Mrs. Latham shook her head. "I need you to help me man the fort around here while everyone's gone. We still have lessons to give and horses to take care of. And don't forget, we have to keep an eye on Dancer for Joelle."

"That's right," Joelle said. "I'm counting on you to keep her company today. Besides, you'll get to go to a horse show soon enough. If you keep practicing on Bluebell, one day you might be able to show him. Right, Mom?"

Mrs. Latham nodded. "You can do anything you set your mind to, sweetie."

Jeff smiled. "I want to win ribbons, like Joelle."

Joelle wondered if he'd really be able to over-come his injury enough to show, but then realized that not too many things could stop her horse-crazy family. Not even spinal injuries or a wheel-chair.

"Boy, horse-craziness sure runs in this family," she said.

"It's called hereditary equine insanity," her mother murmured. "It's inescapable."

Joelle pushed back her chair, kissed her mother and brother good-bye, and grabbed the bag of sandwiches. She stepped outside and was immed-iately surrounded by the barn dogs, all clamoring to be fed.

"Have fun, honey," her mother called after her. "And don't worry about Dancer. We'll keep a close watch on her."

Don't worry? thought Joelle, trying not to trip over the dogs. *Worry is my middle name!* But she took a deep breath of the morning air and looked up at the pearly pink clouds in the sky. She'd try not to worry. Down at the barn, she looked in on Dancer. Bending over, she examined the mare's full teats. She frowned as she saw that a waxy buildup had formed. And Dancer's hip looked hollow. The book had said that meant something, didn't it? Joelle couldn't remember. *You're overreacting*, she told herself. Nothing was going to happen that day. Dancer was contentedly chewing her hay and watching Joelle calmly. "Just don't have that baby until I get back," Joelle said to her horse.

The minute she stepped out of Dancer's stall, Laura asked her to help load some saddles. Joelle placed several in the van, then made more trips to load up buckets, bandages, equine first-aid kits, and anything else that would be needed for their day at the show.

By then the horses' manes and tails had all been braided. Laura and some other stable hands were putting shipping boots and hoods on the horses and starting to lead them toward the waiting vans.

"Hey, kiddo, help me with this big lug," Mr. Latham called. He was leading Great Caesar's Ghost. Ghost wore a traveling hood with a leather head bumper to cushion him in case he banged his head. His legs were encased in big green shipping boots. His tail was bandaged to protect his braids, and he was covered from neck to tail with a green blanket bearing the Windswept logo.

With a sigh, Joelle followed her father and the horse out to the van. Ghost was no picnic to load. The huge Thoroughbred snorted when he saw the van and planted his hooves in the grass. He acted like he'd never seen a van before, even though he'd been trailered regularly to shows for the three years he'd been at Windswept.

"I wish he'd been properly trailer-broken from the start so we wouldn't have this problem," her father muttered. "That foal of Dancer's is going to be trailer-broken practically from birth so we don't have to go through this."

He and Joelle took turns cajoling, talking firmly,

and insistently coaxing the horse until he finally walked up the ramp into the van. As she watched him settle in, Joelle thought about the ladylike way Dancer loaded, daintily and with no fuss. Her only requirement was that she be allowed to be by an open window so she could let her head hang out. She enjoyed whuffling in the air as the van made its way toward the horse show. Joelle forced down a big gulp. She hadn't even left Windswept and already she missed Dancer!

By the time all the horses were loaded, a few cars had pulled into the parking lot. Joelle recognized one of them as Nicole's mother's station wagon.

Nicole and Kendra jumped out. They both had on their riding clothes with sweatshirts over their ratcatchers. They carried their hunt coats in garment bags so they wouldn't get dusty. Nicole's hair was pinned up under her velvet hunt cap, but it was already trying to spill out. Kendra looked like a model from a riding-equipment catalog. She was small and delicate and perfectly put together. Her cheeks were flushed with a delicate tinge of pink, her creamy breeches didn't have a speck of dust on them, and her hair was smoothed perfectly under her cap.

"You guys look great," Joelle said admiringly.

"Thanks. I'm so excited," Nicole said. "I hope the jumps are big and gnarly."

"Stop it," Kendra said, nervously toying with her tiny horseshoe earrings. "You're making my stomach do flips. I hope the jumps don't look too huge, or I'll lose my nerve."

While Mr. Latham discussed his instructions with the head groom, the three girls scrambled into one of the vans, hanging up their garment bags and settling in on the big seats.

They took off just as the sun peeked over the hills. Twenty minutes later, they drove through the wrought-iron gates of Oak Meadows Riding Club. Already there was a great deal of activity in the trailer parking area. Joelle and her friends recognized vans from all the local stables.

They hopped out, waved to their friends, and set to work unloading Windswept's horses. There was no time to waste. Nicole tacked up Valor and immediately followed Mr. Latham over to the schooling ring. Her class was first. Joelle busied herself helping other riders tack up and climb aboard. It seemed like she fastened a million straps, adjusted even more girths, and dusted off a zillion boots. Soon everyone who had morning classes had mounted and headed off to the schooling ring.

Joelle walked over to the rails and watched as her father gave last-minute instructions to the Windswept students. She was glad to see that Nicole looked relaxed. Valor was moving out easily. Nicole did her warmup exercises, and soon took a few practice fences in the middle of the schooling ring.

Joelle saw Kendra warming Chips up on the flat

course, and she smiled. Her smile turned into a frown when Devin Butler entered the ring on his dark bay horse, Blade Runner.

Don't you dare start causing trouble, she thought with annoyance. Devin seemed particularly tense and angry that day, hunched over toward the front of his saddle. He needed to relax and go with the motion of his horse. Joelle winced as she heard Devin snap at his trainer. The trainer yelled back at him. Joelle couldn't help wondering how Devin's riding might improve if her father could train him for a while.

What am I thinking? Joelle stopped herself. *He's a troublemaker. Anyway, he's with Oak Meadows—our competition.* She wished she and Dancer were in top form. They'd show him a thing or two about working as a team!

Just then the P.A. crackled with the announcement that the first class, hunters over fences, would begin in ten minutes. The rest of the day was a blur to Joelle as she ran between the rings and the van, calling riders to get over to the schooling ring, congratulating Windswept riders who were victorious in their classes, and consoling others who weren't having a good day. She transferred saddles, changed bridles, walked horses, and dusted off more boots. She tried to get over to watch Nicole's hunter class, but just as Nicole was about to go, one of the horses tied to the van spooked, and Joelle had to go calm him down.

In the early afternoon she finally had time to

take a break and was grateful when Laura brought her a lemonade from the concession stand.

"Guess what? Nicole won her equitation-over-fences class! She's in second place for the championship, and Windswept is tied with Oak Meadows for the most points!" Laura announced. "Jumper stakes is starting right now."

Joelle gulped her drink, thanked Laura, and took off for the ring. She watched with pride as her father won the jumper stakes on Great Caesar's Ghost, and she waited for Nicole's final class of the day. This class would determine the championship.

"We've just got to win! Come on, Nicole," Kendra breathed in Joelle's ear as the two girls leaned against the rail.

The final class was a flat class, which meant that there would be no jumping, so there would be many horses and riders in the ring at one time. Joelle watched in dismay as Valor got crowded at the rail by another horse and shortened his stride at the canter. "Hold him steady, Nicole," she murmured desperately, mentally riding along with her best friend. But Nicole wasn't the rider Joelle was. She couldn't get Valor to go smoothly in the crowded ring. Joelle watched as Devin rode by on his other horse, Megaton. He looked perfect. Well, except for the way he hunched. Still, the judge nodded at him and marked something on his clipboard. Not a good sign for Windswept.

The judge called for a hand gallop, and Joelle

frowned as Nicole tensed up on Valor's mouth. The big horse sped up and Nicole lurched forward on his neck, her foot falling out of the stirrup. Feeling the loose stirrup bang his side, Valor leaped sideways and Nicole tumbled off into the ring.

"Loose horse. Will the riders in the main ring please hold up," the announcer said over the loudspeaker.

Nicole got up and dusted off her breeches, then walked over to grab Valor's reins. "I'm sorry," she said to Mr. Latham as she walked out of the ring gate.

"You'll get it next time," he said, giving her a squeeze on her shoulder. "Don't worry about it. All that matters is that you weren't hurt."

A short while later, the winners were announced. Devin had taken the blue. That meant the championship had gone to Oak Meadows.

"Never mind, Nicole," Joelle called to her friend. Nicole shrugged and took off her hunt cap, freeing her curls. She led Valor toward the van. Joelle watched glumly as Devin Butler took the large gleaming silver trophy from some smiling ladies at the closing ceremony.

"Can you believe it?" Kendra muttered as they walked back to the Windswept van. "We had it sewn up until that last class. And we can't blame it on Devin. He was miles away from Nicole when Valor blew up."

"Well, there's always the next show. Oak

Meadows isn't unbeatable," Joelle said with more conviction than she felt. She was tired and disappointed, and she couldn't wait to get back to Windswept's familiar grounds and to Dancer. She felt guilty about leaving her mare.

The group drove home in silence. Even Joelle's father seemed disappointed. Joelle knew he didn't mind if his riders did their best and didn't win, but when they let a horse get the better of them the way Nicole had, he didn't like it a bit.

It was well after dark when they pulled into Windswept's driveway. Instantly, Joelle recognized Dr. Butler's truck pulled up next to the old barn. Why was his truck there? Was one of the horses sick or injured?

Or maybe—although Joelle didn't dare to dream it after such a disappointing day—maybe Dancer was having her foal!

Four

THE HORSE VAN HAD BARELY COME TO A HALT BEFORE Joelle threw open the door, hurled herself out of the cab, and tore down the path leading to the barn. Force of habit made her slow down once she got inside the barn. "No running when horses are around." Her father's voice rang in her ears—he had been telling her that for years.

In spite of her best efforts to move quietly, her boot heels rapped sharply on the cement aisle. If Dancer was foaling, she didn't want to disturb her. When she approached her horse's stall, she saw Dr. Butler standing inside. As Joelle got closer the vet turned toward her and raised his finger to his lips. "Easy there, girl," he murmured. Joelle couldn't tell whether he said that for her benefit or for Dancer's.

He shook his head in response to Joelle's questioning look, then stepped out of the stall. "Not yet. But she's just about there. Your mother and brother have been watching her all afternoon. I just got here a little while ago and checked her over. All systems go, though Dancer's having a bit of a hard time. Not too unusual in a maiden mare."

Joelle looked in the stall. Dancer's tail had been bandaged tightly. Her father had told her that would be done when the time came to make the foal's delivery easier. The shavings had been removed from the stall and replaced by straw. Dancer's neck had broken out in a sweat, and Joelle could see the sheen of her sweaty black flanks. Now the mare was pacing around her stall and licking the walls.

"Dancer," the girl murmured softly. Dancer glanced her way for a moment, but then went back to her self-appointed task of licking the walls.

"Why is she doing that?" Joelle asked, just as her father slipped up behind her with Nicole and Kendra in tow. The three of them and the groom had unloaded the horses as quickly as they could without spooking them. They were excited about Dancer's foaling and wanted to watch, too.

"She's expending nervous energy. Poor old girl. She knows something is up, but doesn't quite know what. You know, I've seen lots of horses give birth," Dr. Butler said, never taking his eyes off the mare, "but there isn't one of them that's exactly the same as the others."

"How much longer?"

"Hard to say. Not much, I suppose."

"Is there anything we can do to make her feel better?" Joelle asked anxiously. It was awful to see her horse so agitated.

When Dr. Butler shook his head, Joelle leaned against the stall bars and watched helplessly.

"She could go on like this for quite a while," Dr. Butler said. "All we can do at this point is watch and wait."

After a bit, Joelle was vaguely aware that her father and her friends were moving away from the stall. "We're going to finish the unloading. You can stay here," her father said.

Joelle smiled gratefully and turned back to Dancer. She didn't want to leave the mare's side for even a minute.

"Isn't it exciting?" Nicole said to her as she led Valor into his stall a few minutes later.

Joelle could only nod. She'd been waiting for over eleven months, and now the moment was at hand. If only Dancer would have an easy time of it. She hadn't realized how uncomfortable the mare would look just before giving birth. She closed her eyes. *Please, please, let the foal be okay,* she chanted to herself as she watched Dancer. She began to lose track of time and hardly heard as her friends called good night.

Joelle shoved her hands in her pockets and leaned her head against the stall bars. Finally she paced up and down the barn aisle to pass the time, but it still seemed like forever before anything happened. Her father stepped out of Ghost's stall, saw Joelle, and dropped his arm around her shoulders. The two walked back to Dancer's stall.

Dr. Butler shook his head. "Not yet."

"We'll be up all night with this foaling business. Let's go up to the house and have some dinner," Mr. Latham said wearily.

Joelle shook her head.

"Well, I'm going. I'll be back in a while. Come up when you get tired, or buzz me from the office if you want to bunk out on the couch. I can bring dinner down if you want. Can I get you dinner or coffee or anything, Gerald?"

The vet nodded. "Coffee would be great. I think it's going to be a long night."

Dr. Butler pulled a bale of hay in front of Dancer's stall and sat down. Joelle continued to pace, and finally she could stand it no longer. "When will something happen? This is awful!"

Dr. Butler's face lit up in a slow smile. "Patience. I know it's hard, but Mother Nature has her own timetable."

Joelle groaned and looked in on Dancer. "Do you think she'll be okay? Do you think the foal will be okay?"

The vet looked at her thoughtfully. "We have no reason to think otherwise right now."

Joelle felt reassured. After a while, she sat on the hay bale next to the vet. Soon her head started to feel heavy, and she leaned slowly toward Dr. Butler's shoulder. . . .

"Coffee, Gerald?" Joelle's eyes flew open at the sound of her mother's voice.

"Thanks," the vet said, taking a steaming cup from Mrs. Latham.

Then her mother reached out to pull Joelle up. "Let's get you up to bed, miss."

"No," Joelle protested, trying to stifle a yawn. She had to be there when her horse foaled. She just had to!

Suddenly, they all heard a rustling from the stall. Dr. Butler set his coffee down and he and Joelle stood up. They watched as Dancer started walking in small circles and eventually sank down in the stall.

"Look at her sides heaving," Mrs. Latham said. "Contractions."

Joelle couldn't take her eyes off her mare. Dr. Butler slowly opened the stall door, then stepped inside. Joelle felt her heart pound as she listened to Dancer groan softly. Little rivers of sweat began pouring off the horse's hide.

"You're okay," Joelle said lovingly to her horse.

A short while later she saw Dr. Butler lean over by Dancer's tail and gently start to work a glistening sac outward. Joelle stood on the hay bale and watched as two small forefeet put in their appearance, then a nose, then a whole tiny, exquisite foal!

"A filly!" pronounced Dr. Butler. He stood back as a proud Dancer bent her head around and started licking the wet, black lump. She stopped for a moment to neigh softly.

"A filly," Joelle repeated with wonder. "A filly!" Dancer had done it!

Joelle's mother leaned over and gave her daughter a hug. "A filly! I'll go call Jeff and your dad." She raced off for the barn office.

Joelle was mesmerized. She'd never seen anything so wonderful in her entire life. Dancer had given birth to a filly! And what a filly. She was perfect. She was glistening black and had tiny teacup hooves, a fuzzy stump of a tail, and—

"A perfect white star, just like Dancer's!" she breathed.

"She's a beauty, all right," Dr. Butler said. "Just like her mama."

"And she didn't have a complicated delivery after all!" Joelle let out her breath in a whoosh of relief.

Dancer licked and whuffled softly to her foal, gently urging her to stand. By the time Mrs. Latham came back with Jeff, Dancer was standing up and drying off her baby. Joelle's father and Jeff arrived just as the foal shook herself off and struggled to rise to her feet. She wobbled for a second or two, then gave a great big heave and stood up, breathing heavily with exertion. Then she looked up at her audience as if to say, "Didn't I do well?"

"Isn't she beautiful?" Joelle asked, her eyes shining. "Oh, good work, Dancer!"

"Hooray, hooray. She finally had her baby!" Jeff

yelled as he spun his wheelchair around in circles. Suddenly he realized he was being left out. "Hey, I can't see! I can't see!" he protested.

Mr. Latham lifted him out of his wheelchair so he could see Dancer and the filly.

"She's so little," breathed Jeff.

"Not for long," Dr. Butler said, standing back now that his work was finished. "This little baby's going to grow fast. Give her love and she'll thrive." He turned to Joelle. "No shortage of that with you around, I'll bet."

Joelle nodded. How could she not love something as wondrous as this delicate little creature before her?

"I hope she starts nursing soon," Joelle's father said.

Joelle turned to face her father and put her hands on her hips. "Geez, Dad. She's only just been born, and already she's standing up. Why rush things?"

Mr. Latham raised his eyebrows. "You've done enough reading to know that it's important that the mare let down her milk right away."

"Why?" Jeff asked.

"The foal needs her first milk," Joelle explained to Jeff. "It's called colostrum, and it's full of antibodies that the foal will need to fight off infection."

"That's it, folks," Dr. Butler said, stepping out of the stall. "Now Dancer has to take over. This is all we can do."

"What are you going to name her, Joelle?" Jeff

said from his perch in Mr. Latham's arms.

Joelle looked blank. "I don't know. I think I'll wait until I get to know her better. Dancer and I will think of something, won't we, girl?"

The group stood gathered around the stall and watched for a few more minutes as Dancer nudged the foal toward her bulging teats. Finally the foal started sucking.

"Whew! That part always worries me," said Joelle's father with a relieved sigh. "I've seen mares before who for some reason don't let down their milk. And it's a real hassle bottle-feeding a foal."

"Well, guys, let's get to bed. We'll need our strength for tomorrow," Joelle's mother said.

"Awwww," Jeff protested as Mr. Latham set him back in his chair.

"I'll stay here just a while longer," Dr. Butler said, sitting down on his bale again.

"Me, too," Joelle said.

Mrs. Latham shook her head. "It's late. You're going to bed, young lady."

Joelle frowned and looked at the vet.

"Don't worry. I'll stay here to keep an eye on things," he added, winking at her.

Just as the Lathams reached the end of the barn aisle, Joelle heard a snorting, then a groan. She turned around anxiously as she saw Dr. Butler leap to his feet. He rushed over to the stall door and threw it open.

"What's going on?" Joelle asked, fear gripping her heart like an icy, monstrous hand.

"I'm not sure," her father said. "You stay here."

"Joelle—" Her mother grabbed her by the arm to keep her from following Mr. Latham. Something was wrong! The foal was in trouble. She had to go help her!

"What's happening?" Jeff asked.

No one answered. It seemed an eternity that Joelle stood there, listening to the rustling in Dancer's stall. If someone didn't say something soon, she was going to scream!

Finally, her father emerged from Dancer's stall. His shoulders were slumped. Dr. Butler followed him.

"What's happening?" Joelle finally shrieked.

"Deborah, take the kids to the house," Mr. Latham said shortly.

Joelle's mother put an arm around her shoulder, but Joelle pulled away and ran toward the two men. "What is it? What's happened to the foal?"

Dr. Butler looked at the ground. Her father's eyes met hers. She could see a sheen in them. Was he crying? What had happened? She tried to push past him toward the stall, but he grabbed her by the shoulders to stop her.

"Joelle," he said at last. "Listen to me."

"The foal! Is she dead? What is it? Dad, tell me!" she yelled, trying to squirm out of his arms.

"Joelle, honey, it couldn't be helped. It's no one's fault."

"It happens sometimes," Dr. Butler said. "Rarely, but it happens."

Joelle stood back and took a big gulp of air. "Tell me."

"Joelle, Dancer was hemorrhaging very badly."

She heard a roaring in her ears that grew louder and louder. She clapped her hands over them, trying to keep out her father's words. But she couldn't.

"Dr. Butler—" He paused and swallowed hard. "Dr. Butler had to put her down."

It must be some mistake, Joelle thought. *Some hideous mistake.* Dancer wasn't dead. She couldn't be.

Joelle's father embraced her hard. She let herself flop into his strong arms. *No. No. No. This is some horrible nightmare. Some late-night horror movie.*

But then she pulled away and looked at the weary faces of the two men. It was true. Dancer, her beloved horse, was dead!

"I hope the foal makes it," Dr. Butler said.

"The foal? You're worried about the foal? The foal that killed my Dancer? I don't care what happens to that stupid foal! I'll never forgive her!"

Tears blinding her, Joelle spun around and ran away from the barn, away from the lifeless form in Dancer's stall, away from the awful foal, and out into the black night.

Five

JOELLE WAS RUNNING AS FAST AS SHE COULD. HER SIDES began to ache and her head was pounding, but she kept running, out of the barn, and up the path to the house. She couldn't let the horror of what had just happened catch up with her. If she ran faster and faster, maybe she could outrun it. Throwing open the back door, she bolted for her bedroom. Without turning on the lights, she hurtled into her room and threw herself down on the floor of her closet, slamming the door behind her.

It was okay. It was dark. It was quiet. It was black nothingness. There was no death. No pain. No past, present, or future. Only a still void stretching into infinity. Joelle lay without thinking for hours. Finally, the blackness surrounded her and she slept.

Joelle had no idea how long she was in the

bonds of the blackness, but slowly it released its hold on her. She became aware that there was a sliver of light coming under her closet door. Joelle stood up, kicked her riding boots aside, and emerged from the closet. Sunlight was pouring into the room, stinging her eyes, shocking her senses. *What was I doing in my closet?* Her mind struggled to make sense of it, and when it did, the full memory of the previous night's horror flung itself cruelly into her face. The triumphant birth of a black, fuzzy bundle of wonder. Dancer's proud nicker of "See? I did it!" A foal standing up and nursing for the first time. The dull thump of a horse going down. The hushed whispers of the vet.

But the horror movie that played in eerie slow motion through Joelle's brain had no power over her. *My horse is not dead. That did not happen,* Joelle told herself firmly. She was there in her room with pictures of Dancer surrounding her. Dancer's bridle was still slung over her chair, just like always. That meant Dancer was outside. She would go down and eat breakfast and head to the barn, and Dancer would be waiting for her, just like always—

It was better not to think beyond the fact that it was Monday. A school day. Joelle moved like a robot through her shower. Mechanically, she put on her school clothes, a stiff white blouse and a denim skirt. Her hair seemed to brush itself into a ponytail. Her hands and arms were not part of her

62

as they gathered up her backpack and shoved her textbooks in. Her feet moved down the hallway and down the stairs with a mind of their own.

When her gray-faced parents greeted her at the breakfast table with concerned looks and murmurs, Joelle's voice spoke on its own. "Hi. I'm fine. Really. You don't have to look so worried."

Her mouth willed the words "What's for breakfast?" and "Where's Jeff?" but Joelle didn't hear the answers. Her mouth chewed whatever it was that her mother placed in front of her, but Joelle couldn't taste a thing.

She stood up automatically at the sound of the school bus horn. "Good-bye, Dad, Mom." She leaned over to kiss first her mother, then her father. Her father caught her shoulders and forced her to sit back down.

"Joelle, it's okay if you don't want to go to school today," he said, looking into her dull eyes. "Joelle— where do I begin? What do I say?"

"There's nothing to say." Joelle's voice sounded flat, even to herself. "Dad, I'm old enough to know how it works. Horses are born, they live, they die."

Mr. Latham ran his hand through his hair and managed a sad smile. "Was that one of my famous lectures?" He sighed and shook his head. "I used to think I knew all the answers when it came to horses, but now I don't know what to say."

Joelle stood up again. "You don't have to say anything," she repeated. "I'm okay. I mean, sure, I'm—uh—sad. Is that what you wanted to hear?

But I have to go to school. See? There's the horn again."

Without waiting for an answer, Joelle grabbed her backpack and ran out the door. She headed down the driveway and clambered aboard the bus. She took an empty seat near the back of the bus.

A couple of stops later, Nicole came aboard. She made her way down the narrow aisle, her book bag banging against every seat. Her eyes were sparkling, and the second she was within earshot, she breathed, "Well, tell me everything! It's so exciting! Did Dancer do it? Did she foal? Come on! I'm dying to know everything."

Joelle nodded and looked at the floor. Hmm. She'd put on two different-colored shoes. Actually, they looked pretty good together. Two unmatched sneakers. That was okay. Nothing else made sense, either.

"Hey, Joelle." Nicole's voice got a funny catch in it. She laid her hand gently on Joelle's sleeve. "Is—is the foal okay?"

Joelle conjured up the black bundle's face with its familiar white star. She nodded. "The foal is just fine."

Nicole was silent. Waiting. Waiting. Joelle glanced at her friend's curly dark hair. *She really should wear it up,* she thought. Trailing down the way it did over Nicole's shoulders, it looked, well, untamed somehow. She shook her head to clear her mind of thoughts about Nicole's hair. Wasn't Nicole saying something to her? Shouldn't she be listening?

"Hey, are you on another planet or something?" Nicole asked with concern.

"No. I'm right here. Yeah, Dancer had her foal. Sorry," Joelle said. The horror threatened to bubble up in her throat again, but at Joelle's command, it worked its way back down deep inside her.

"That's okay," Nicole said.

Kendra got on at the next stop. She opened her mouth to talk to Joelle, but when she saw the look on her face and glanced at Nicole, her mouth closed again.

The bus dropped everyone off in front of school. There was a blur of lockers, a bell that sounded far off. A round of classes began. Joelle didn't remember how she ended up in her seat in history class. She didn't notice that Devin shot her a look of surprise when she entered the classroom. She didn't make a move when Devin thumped a football-shaped note on her desk a few minutes later. She didn't hear him whisper, "Hey, Joelle, I'm really sorry," when Mrs. Rubins turned her back for a minute.

She only half listened as the teacher started her lecture about the French and Indian War. War. Joelle hated thinking about it. She winced as she opened her textbook to the class reading. There were illustrations of the battles. One picture showed a soldier being shot. His horse was going down in a swirl of dust, its eyes wide and terrified. Suddenly, the horror rose up unbidden in Joelle's throat. She sat up straight and Dancer's image leaped in front of her eyes. It swirled around and around, faster and faster. Joelle's hand shot up.

"May I be excused?" she heard her strangled voice cry.

Mrs. Rubins understood at once that something was wrong. "Yes. Do you need some assistance?" Without waiting for an answer, she then asked, "Devin, would you please see that Joelle makes it to the nurse's office?"

Joelle didn't want Devin to take her to the nurse, but there seemed no point in resisting. She had to get outside before the classroom air choked her. She left his football-shaped note on her desk and hurried out of the classroom. She and the vet's son walked down the hall in silence. After a bit, he reached out and put his hand on her arm, as if to guide her.

"I'm okay. Really," she said, trying to jerk her arm away. "It's just that my horse died and my head hurts and I don't want to think about some stupid war right now."

There. The horror was out.

"I know," Devin said quietly. "My dad told me. I'm sorry. But I couldn't believe you'd be at school."

"I don't think I should have come," came Joelle's halting words. "I'm going home."

The two paused outside the door of the nurse's office. "Thank you, Devin. Really, I'm okay."

She walked inside, and the next thing she knew, she was being held in Mrs. Goodall's strong arms and lifted gently onto a gray-blanketed cot.

Joelle couldn't tell how much later it was that her mother was standing over her, saying, "I never should have let you try to come to school."

Joelle allowed herself to be led out to the car. And once she hit the cool seat, the hot tears came.

"I know, baby, I know," Mrs. Latham said over and over during the ride home. She stroked Joelle's arm while keeping her eyes on the road.

"Dancer! Dancer!" The words hurled themselves out of Joelle's mouth. She was vaguely aware that the car had pulled up in front of the house. Her body continued to shake with sobs, and her mother held her tightly. Finally, she was able to get out of the car.

"I'm sorry," Joelle said.

"You don't have to be sorry for your feelings," her mother said. "Let's go inside." Joelle let her mother seat her at the table and bring her some soothing herbal tea.

"Where's Jeff?" she asked.

"He came home early from school, too. He's— he's down at the barn." Her eyes searched Joelle's face.

"I'm going to go watch TV," Joelle announced abruptly. She wandered into the living room and flipped on the set. And before long, she slept.

She was roused a couple of hours later when her mother came into the room with Jeff. Jeff wheeled his chair up to the couch where his sister lay sprawled.

"Dad was worried about the foal," he said

matter-of-factly. "I was just down there singing to her. She likes it."

Joelle didn't respond.

"You know, Joelle, another thing we're going to have to face is the fact that motherless foals often don't make it," her mother added.

Joelle still didn't respond.

"Dr. Butler will be up at the house in a few minutes. He just trailered over a mare that had a stillbirth. Her name's Blossom. We made an arrangement with her owners. She's got plenty of milk, so she's going to wet-nurse your foal. The foal got Dancer's colostrum, but she needs more than that."

As if she cared. Joelle shook her head. "Doesn't matter."

Her mother stood up and put her hands on her slim hips. "Yes, it does matter. It matters a great deal." She paused. "She needs love and care."

Love? thought Joelle in dismay. *Love hurts too much. I have no more love.*

There was a knock at the back door, and Jeff wheeled out to answer it. Dr. Butler came into the living room. He looked tired and uneasy.

Joelle sat up. "Hi," she said.

"Your filly took to the wet nurse right away," he said.

"Oh."

Dr. Butler sat down in a chair across from Joelle. After a minute he spoke. "I'm sorry about Dancer. I wish I could have saved her," he said.

Joelle stared at the carpet. "It wasn't your fault. The filly killed her."

"Joelle, you know that's not the case," Dr. Butler said. "Foals don't kill mares. An artery in Dancer's uterus burst."

Joelle shuddered.

"I know it's shocking," Dr. Butler said. "But you need to hear the truth, however painful. It was a fluke. It was not the filly's fault. I know you need to cry over your loss, but you also have to get on with the business of raising that foal."

Joelle shook her head.

The vet's voice dropped almost to a whisper. "I know you know about my daughter. When she was taken from us, I thought I'd never smile again. It takes some time, but you learn to go on. Even Devin's beginning to see this."

Joelle could think of nothing to say.

The vet stood up and patted her shoulder. "I've got to run now. I've got another call to make. I'll be back to check on the foal a little later."

After Dr. Butler left, Joelle pressed her face into the couch and let her tears flow again.

A couple of days slipped by where Joelle did nothing. She didn't bother to get up for school. Her friends stopped by once or twice and called. Nicole sent a goofy get-well card, and Kendra brought over some homemade chocolate chip cookies. Joelle could barely remember her conversations with them.

She remembered her bad dreams, though,

especially the one where she was riding Dancer, galloping joyously in the sun. Then, suddenly, Dancer was gone; she'd disappeared from under her. And Joelle was running through a brown, dry pasture, a small black foal chasing her. She had woken up with tears streaming down her cheeks.

One cloudy morning she woke up to find her father sitting on the edge of her bed, just watching her.

"There's a foal out there who misses Dancer as much as you do. Jeff's been out there every day since her birth, but she could use some of your love, too," he said quietly. "I think she's going to make it. She's taken to the wet nurse, but still . . ."

"Dad, I miss Dancer so much," Joelle wailed. She hugged her pillow to her chest and stared at the ceiling.

Her father shrugged and stood up. Then he walked over to Joelle's bulletin board and looked for a moment at the photos and ribbons.

"Remember when you and Dancer took the blue at the Spring Valley schooling show when you were only eight?" he asked, gazing at the faded, wrinkled photograph of Joelle with a huge smile, holding a giant rosette. His eyes moved on to a photo of Joelle in a blue hunt coat standing proudly next to Dancer, who was covered with the championship blanket they'd just won. "Or the time when you made off with the medal at the Camelot hunter-jumper show? I was so proud of you and Dancer that day."

Joelle turned her head toward her bulletin board

and looked at the picture of herself standing next to Dancer in front of Windswept's barn. "Yeah," she said quietly. "I could never forget any of those things."

Her father turned back to face her. "I guess that's my point. You've got Dancer and the things you two did together locked firmly in your heart. Nothing can take that from you. Not death, not anything."

"So?" Joelle challenged her father, still hugging her pillow.

"So Dancer's still alive in your heart. Now you have to hold her memory close and get out there and live some more. Believe me, honey, in your lifetime you'll see plenty of great horses come and go—"

Joelle flinched and her father stopped. He raised his hands in a gesture of helplessness.

Joelle didn't move. Finally her father mumbled something about having to go supervise the workers on the new barn. "And this afternoon, we're trailering in a couple of new school horses. I think you'll like them."

"I guess so," Joelle said because she knew it was expected of her. She sat up and made a move to get out of bed. It was hard. There didn't seem to be much point.

"Get dressed. Come on down," her father said as he left the room.

She stood in the shower a long time, her mind replaying some of the highlights of her years with Dancer. The horse shows, the long afternoon trail rides, the quiet talks in the barn. The summer days before the drought when she and Dancer would splash and play in the creek. The tears came again, and Joelle felt as if the stream of water was washing away her memories.

After she dressed, she headed downstairs. Her mother and Jeff were in the kitchen. Jeff was sitting at the table playing a hand-held video game while he ate breakfast. Her mother was wearing her riding clothes. She looked tired and worn.

"Morning, pumpkin," she said. "Waffle?"

Joelle nodded and got a plate from the cupboard.

"Your face is all red, Joelle," Jeff announced. "You've been crying for days."

Joelle glared at him. He looked ridiculously happy, playing with his game without a worry in the world.

"You'd cry, too, if you lost everything you ever loved!" she spat out.

"I lost Dancer, too," Jeff pointed out. "And I didn't turn into a mean monster like you."

Joelle could feel her anger boil to the surface. "Well, I don't care what you think. Dancer was just another horse to you, but to me, she was everything! What do you know, anyway, Jeff?"

"More than you do," Jeff shot back. "I know what it feels like to feed a baby foal a bottle. And to watch her chase her shadow. And Laura let me help put her halter on for the first time. You haven't seen her at all. You can't know anything about foals. You just stay in your stupid room and cry."

"Leave me alone," Joelle said. She stabbed her waffle viciously with her fork.

"Enough, you two," Mrs. Latham interrupted. "Joelle, Jeff has the day off, but I'll drive you to school. You missed the bus."

"I'm not going to school," Joelle snapped.

"You *are* going to school," her mother said firmly. "Honey, I know you're hurting. Believe me, if there were something I could do to get Dancer back, I'd do it. I've cried, too. She was a magnificent horse, and I'm going to miss her like crazy. But we've got to go on. Now, we've let you handle it your own way for a few days. But you've missed a fair amount of school, and your grades are important. It's time to get back into the swing of things."

Joelle looked up moodily from her breakfast and pushed her plate away. She said nothing, but got up and got her backpack.

Her mother and Jeff chatted cheerily all the way to school. When they pulled up in front of Fire Canyon Middle School, Joelle got out and slammed the door. Still, when she started making her way through the crowded halls to her locker, she felt a little better. School was safe. It had nothing to do with horses. It didn't hurt. For the moment, that was enough.

"Joelle, I think Devin likes you," Nicole announced when her friends met her at her locker. "He asked about you every day when you were home."

Joelle saw Kendra step on Nicole's toe. "Nicole," Kendra hissed.

Joelle shook her head. "His dad told him to do that," she muttered. And actually, the thought annoyed her.

She avoided Devin's eyes during history. For the next few periods, she tried to pay attention to the class discussions. It was better than letting her mind wander to things she didn't want to think about.

At lunchtime, Nicole started telling some long, impossible story. The other girls at the lunch table laughed, but Joelle sat mechanically chewing her sandwich. The story just didn't seem that funny to her. After a while, Joelle noticed that her friends were talking about math, the school dance, sports, anything but horses. That was fine with her. She just wanted school to be over. Then she could go home and watch TV and stop thinking.

On the bus on the way home, she just looked out the window. When she got out with all the lesson kids, she noticed that Nicole didn't head for her house as usual.

"We're going down to the barn. Your mother said the lesson would start at three thirty on the dot," Nicole said awkwardly.

Joelle didn't look at her friends. She concentrated instead on Wolfie and Carpy, who were now gamboling toward her. "Fine, guys, see ya," she said, kicking at the dirt.

"You're coming down later, then?" Kendra asked hopefully.

"No," Joelle said.

She turned and walked into her house, into the safety of her room, far, far away from horses.

But she couldn't escape them. After Joelle dumped her books on her bed, she caught a glimpse of her bulletin board, covered with photos of Dancer and ticket stubs from grand prix jumping events she'd been to. Her eyes moved to the rows of model horses lined up on her windowsills, then on to the bridle waiting expectantly over her chair. Horses and reminders of horses were everywhere. Memories of Dancer were everywhere—only the mare was gone and she wasn't ever coming back.

Joelle sprang into action. She wasn't going to be hurt by horses ever again! Moving swiftly, fueled by a rage burning deep inside her, she pulled off photo after photo, ticket after ticket, premium after premium. Down came the ribbons proudly hanging from the lamp next to her bed. The model horses found a new home in her closet, shoved unceremoniously on top of old stuffed animals and board games. Dancer's bridle was heaved on the floor of her closet, behind her shoes.

When she was done, Joelle stood with her hands on her hips and looked around her bare room. It looked weird. Empty. But that matched her mood these days. She slumped on her bed. Maybe her mother would let her redecorate it one day. Maybe she could get new wallpaper, like some of the other girls had. New lacquered furniture. Something more grown-up. It was time to put away her little-girl dreams of horses.

But still her room looked bare. Its blank walls made her feel like she didn't really belong there. After a few minutes, she headed downstairs and out the kitchen door. She didn't head toward the barn, but rather turned round toward the front of the house. She plopped herself on the front lawn and stared out at the highway running past the house. That way she couldn't see any of Wind-swept's barns. She could pretend horses didn't exist.

After a while, she felt a cool nose press itself into her hand. Wolfie, the barn dog, crept into her lap. He snuffled and licked her face. Joelle petted him without thinking.

Oh, Dancer, Dancer, she cried silently, burying her face into Wolfie's coarse coat.

Would it ever stop hurting?

Six

FOR THE NEXT FEW DAYS, JOELLE DRAGGED HERSELF
through school, then went to her room for the rest
of the day. It wasn't until Saturday that she finally
found the strength to force herself to see the
horses. She hadn't intended to go outside, but
sitting in the empty kitchen, Joelle had decided
that being alone all day was too much to bear.
There'd been too many lonely days lately.

Joelle was surprised to find the barn nearly
deserted. Walking down the aisle, Joelle turned
her eyes away from Dancer's stall. She stepped
outside and saw that the rings were empty and
there were no horses cavorting around the paddocks. Normally, by this hour the first lessons
would be over and the barn would be filled with
the sounds of riders washing their horses down.
But that day, it was quiet.

Concerned, Joelle trotted a little faster through B Barn. All the horses were in their stalls, blanketed, some dozing on their feet with their heads low. What was going on?

Behind the barn, Joelle spied a group of students gathered around her father. He had a poster of a horse propped on an easel and was pointing with a long stick to the labeled parts of the body.

"Poll, throatlatch, cheekbone, muzzle," his voice droned, and his students' voices chorused after him.

Mr. Latham was giving one of his "chalk talks," as he called them. That was odd. Normally he saved this sort of off-the-horse lesson for days when it was too windy or too cold to ride. But that afternoon was warm and beautiful, without a hint of the Santa Ana winds that sometimes roared through Windswept's valley.

"What's going on?" Joelle whispered to Nicole, kneeling next to her friend.

Nicole looked up with surprise. "Oh, I'm so glad you're here. We're having a conformation lesson."

"I know it's a conformation lesson. But why? It's a perfect Saturday. Everyone should be riding."

"Dr. Butler came by yesterday and gave all the horses their flu vaccines, so they can't be ridden today," Nicole told her.

"Usually *you're* the one telling *us* when the horses are getting their shots," Kendra whispered.

"Boy, you really are out of it."

Joelle shrugged. "Maybe I am."

Just then, Joelle's father shot them a warning glance. His eyes rested briefly on Joelle, then he turned back to his chart.

"Gaskin, point of hock, hock," he continued, his stick pointing to the pictured horse's hind legs.

"Where's my mother?" Joelle dared to whisper a few minutes later.

"She's over by the hot walker giving a grooming demonstration to the beginners," Kendra answered.

Joelle headed toward the hot walker, a machine that automatically walked the horses in circles to cool them down. Mrs. Latham was holding Bluebell at the end of his lead, while Jeff, in his wheelchair, demonstrated the use of the dandy brush. The little kids were gathered around.

"Now we never, ever use a metal comb on horses' manes or tails, because it will break the delicate hairs," Mrs. Latham was saying. She looked up and flashed Joelle a smile, then turned back to her discussion of manes. "We always patiently separate the hairs, just like your mother does for you when you get tangles."

Several of the little girls giggled.

Joelle shoved her hands in her pockets and slipped away from the group, walking into the new barn. The workers had made a lot of progress since she'd last been down there. The stalls were finished, and there were new horses with unfamiliar names. It was weird how much had gone on without her—and without Dancer.

Joelle sighed and flung herself down on a hay bale. Inhaling deeply, she took in the smell of horses and sawdust. Normally it was a warm, welcoming scent, but that day it didn't seem to have much to do with her.

Suddenly, she heard a shrill little whinny. It was a thin, wobbly sound, like that of a feeble bugler. Joelle jumped up and looked into the stall behind her. She found herself staring into a black, fuzzy foal face.

Dancer's foal!

Joelle's heart closed like a fist in her chest. The foal looked at her, her liquid brown eyes imploring. Joelle coolly studied the foal's familiar white star, her fuzzy tuft of forelock, her scrawny chest, and her long, spindly legs. The foal returned her stare without blinking, her nostrils whuffling in and out at the foreign smell of the stranger before her. Then she turned and moved toward a big shadow in the corner of the stall.

Joelle could see a brown mare standing protectively over the foal. *Must be the wet nurse,* she thought. *Blossom, isn't it? Boy, she looks ancient.* She had a swayback, and her hooves were the size of soup plates. Dancer she was not!

"Isn't she beautiful?" Jeff's voice came from behind her.

Joelle whirled around to see her brother approaching.

"Hardly!" she chortled, turning back to look into the stall again. "Talk about old and sway-backed—"

"I was talking about the foal, horse breath!" Jeff cut in. "And anyway, Blossom is a great mother. The filly loves her."

"Stop calling me horse breath," snapped Joelle.

"You call me cookie breath," Jeff countered.

"Well, she's awfully skinny. The filly, I mean," Joelle said, turning her back on the foal.

"She won't be skinny for long," Jeff challenged her. "I help Mom and Dad give her bottles. Laura bottle-feeds her, too."

Joelle shrugged. She didn't care. She probably shouldn't have come down to the barn, anyway. The foal was a stinging reminder that Dancer was dead.

"Hey, Joelle!" Nicole and Kendra were striding toward her, their riding boots ringing sharply against the concrete.

"I'm so glad you came down to the barn today. I brought you a present," Nicole said. "I've waited weeks to give it to you. I bought it before—before, uh, she was born because I just knew she was going to be a filly." She held out a package wrapped in pink paper. "I know that you're sad about Dancer and all, but I saw this at the tack store, and I couldn't resist it. It was too cute." Nicole was talking fast. Too fast.

Joelle reluctantly took the package. She flinched when she saw the wrapping paper, which was printed with little pink and blue balloons and the word *Congratulations.* She didn't think that the foal's birth should resemble a celebration in any way. But she didn't want to hurt Nicole's feelings. After all, they had been friends since they had terrorized the stables on Bluebell when they were barely out of diapers. Ripping open the paper, Joelle pulled out a bundle of pink nylon. It was a foal halter. "Thanks," she said tonelessly.

Nicole looked deflated. "Well, I thought it was nice. And the foal needs a halter. You should see the rope thingy that Laura leads her around with. Your dad doesn't like it a bit."

Joelle just nodded.

Kendra kicked at the cement with the toe of her boot. "You know, Joelle, it's not the foal's fault that Dancer died," she burst out. "You shouldn't blame her. She's just a baby."

"Yeah," said Jeff.

Joelle held the halter. "I know that. Everyone tells me that," she muttered. Then tears welled up in her eyes, and she bit her lip. "But if she hadn't been born, Dancer never would have died."

"You wanted to breed her," Nicole pointed out. "The foal didn't ask to be born."

"So it's my fault?" Joelle's head snapped up, and she could feel her cheeks get hot. Great. So she'd killed her own horse by deciding to breed her? Now she felt worse than ever!

"No, that's not what I was trying to say!" Nicole replied. She shook her head. "You know everything I say comes out all wrong. It wasn't your fault at all. It's just that—oh, forget it. Come on, Kendra. We've got to get back."

When her friends had left, Joelle tossed the halter in a heap by the stall.

Jeff glared at Joelle, then called to the filly, "Don't worry. At least I love you." Then he spun around in his chair and wheeled down the barn aisle.

Joelle turned the opposite way and kicked at the halter. Breaking into a run, she bolted up to the house—away from the foal, away from the horses. She didn't belong there anymore.

"All right, everyone," Mr. Latham announced at breakfast the next morning. "We're going to give the horses one more day off, and we're going to go out as a family and have some fun." His eyes twinkled, and he looked around the table expectantly.

"Yeah?" Jeff's face lit up.

Even Joelle was excited. This was out of the ordinary for the Lathams. She couldn't remember the last time the family had taken a whole day off from horses and the riding school.

"I've put Laura in charge of the barn today," Mrs. Latham said, standing up to clear away the breakfast dishes. "Things are quiet. Some of the horses still seem a bit off from their flu shots, so we canceled lessons. Instead, we are going to drive up to Horseshoe Lake, have lunch at that new Mexican restaurant, and rent a boat."

Joelle slumped in her chair and took a long, noisy gulp of milk. Normally, she would have loved a day with her family at the lake. But now not even an outing seemed like much fun.

Still, maybe a change of scenery would be okay. Joelle was sick of school, sick of her barren room, and sick of horses. She felt her spirits rise, and she took extra care getting ready. She selected a navy striped shirt to wear with her best jeans. She French-braided her hair and tied a blue ribbon in it to set it off.

Her father let out a low whistle when she made her appearance downstairs. Her mother looked up from the newspaper she was reading and smiled with approval.

"You look nice, dear," she said.

Joelle could tell her parents were also looking forward to the day off. As they sped down the highway her father sang old sea chanties at the top of his lungs.

"Sixteen men on a dead man's chest," he roared.

Joelle stifled a giggle. It was weird to see her normally stern father cut loose like this. Gone were his riding-lesson frowns and lecturesome ways. He looked young and carefree. Soon her mother and Jeff joined in. Joelle stared out the window, pretending she was bored. But in truth, she actually enjoyed seeing her family so happy. It had been a long time since everyone had seemed so relaxed.

The lake area was already crowded when they

arrived. Everywhere, Joelle could see kids on bikes, men and women jogging, and noisy groups flying kites.

"Look at how low the water is," Mrs. Latham said, pointing to the watermark on the shore. "Will it ever rain again? This drought's gone on long enough."

"Drought or no drought, it's a fine day to take a boat ride," Mr. Latham crowed. "We'll hoist the sails and set out!"

"Oh, Dad," Joelle burst out, "you'd think we were going to pilot an ocean liner, not rent a scrawny old tub on little Horseshoe Lake."

"Girl, you don't have an ounce of imagination in your bones," her father said. He grabbed his wife and swung her around. She giggled. Then he gently lifted Jeff up and carried him to the boat rental place.

After they put on their life preservers, they climbed aboard the little dinghy and pushed away from the dock. Jeff demanded the oars immediately, and Mr. Latham let Jeff place his hands on top of his once they were out in the middle of the lake.

"Jeff, stop rocking the boat. We'll capsize," Mrs. Latham cautioned.

"Wouldn't that be fun?" Jeff said mischievously.

"No!" the Lathams cried together.

While her father rowed, Joelle closed her eyes and let the sun warm her face. She felt the lake waters rocking the little rowboat. *It's not unlike a horse*, she found herself thinking. *Like posting to a trot, one-two-one-two.* And when a jet-ski roared by, the wake felt like the rolling motion of the canter.

After an hour or so out on the water, Mrs. Latham declared that all this seamanship had made her hungry, a declaration that Jeff seconded.

"Dave, what do you say we head to shore for some Mexican food?" Mrs. Latham ventured.

Mr. Latham was still humming his sea chanties, but he nodded and started rowing ashore. "This reminds me of my navy days, but hey, who's got time to look back?" That seemed like good thinking to Joelle. One thing she never wanted to do was look back. Because when she did, she started thinking about Dancer and the little foal who looked way too much like her.

"Joelle, your face looks as though a dark cloud has landed on it," her father said. "You aren't seasick, are you?"

"No."

Joelle waited with her mother and Jeff while her father returned the boat.

"Your father's having a wonderful time," Mrs. Latham murmured, reaching out to smooth back a strand of Joelle's hair.

Joelle took that to mean she'd better not do anything to upset him. She jerked up her chin and resolved not to think of Dancer or the skinny little foal any more that day.

A while later, the Lathams were seated at a table overlooking the lake. They'd just been served a huge plate of enchiladas, and Mr. Latham was amusing them with one of his navy stories. Mrs.

Latham and Jeff laughed like crazy, and even Joelle found herself cracking a smile or two.

When he had finished his story, Mr. Latham looked around at his family, who were still chuckling and dabbing at their eyes with their napkins.

"You know," he said quietly, "it's good that we take the time to laugh like this. Heaven knows this family has had its share of bad luck. We had Jeff's accident . . ." He paused and looked at his son. "But Jeff's riding now, and doing pretty darned well, I might add. And he's going to be out of that wheelchair before we know it."

Jeff nodded his head vigorously. "And I'm gonna be a trainer like you one day," he said.

Mrs. Latham ruffled his hair. "I have no doubt."

Joelle slid down in her seat as her father's glance moved her way. "And most recently, we lost Dancer," Mr. Latham continued. Joelle lowered her eyes. "But we go on. We live and we laugh. And it's okay to be happy again."

Joelle shivered and pulled her jacket tightly around her. Hearing that she should be happy somehow made her sad. It didn't seem right to be laughing when Dancer was gone. It felt disloyal. The fun of the afternoon seemed to fade away, as if a cloud had gone over the sun. All the way home, Joelle was silent.

That night she sat in her room, looking out her window at the stars. She thought about what her father had said at lunch. She wondered if she would ever really be happy again.

It was a different Mr. Latham who sat at the breakfast table the next morning. Dressed in his riding boots and breeches, he didn't much resemble the man who'd sung "Sixteen men on a dead man's chest" just the day before. Joelle took her cereal bowl out of the cupboard mechanically. She also felt like a different person from the girl who'd laughed at her father's jokes.

Mrs. Latham worked on her riding schedule while she sipped her coffee, and Mr. Latham was poring over a new show premium. After a while, he looked up and said, "Pretend you're the trainer. Which classes do you think you should enter your students in?" He slid the premium under Joelle's nose.

Joelle shrugged.

"Joelle, I meant what I said about having to carry on," he told her. Then he reached over and handed her the pink halter and matching lead rope.

"Sweetheart," her mother broke in quietly, "the filly's growing every day. She needs to be halter-broken and broken to lead. You want to be a professional trainer one day? Then you've got to carry on with your duties, even if your heart is breaking."

Joelle jumped up. It was a trap! "I won't do it," she said hotly. "Laura gets paid to manage the horses. Let her do it!"

"She's your filly," Jeff cut in. "You were the one who wanted her."

Mrs. Latham looked at him sternly. "Stay out of this, Jeff." She turned back to her daughter. "This one is non-negotiable, Joelle. You wanted to breed Dancer. And although you never expected what happened to happen, the fact remains that you have a commitment to carry through."

"No way!" Joelle said. "I hate that filly."

It was then that she noticed Jeff crying.

"You're mean," he sobbed. "I'd take care of her if I could."

Joelle looked from Jeff's red, swollen eyes to her parents' cool, steely ones. Furiously, she snatched the halter.

"Fine, I'll keep my end of the bargain. I'll take care of the foal," she burst out. "But I don't have to love her."

Joelle stomped out the kitchen door and let the screen bang loudly behind her.

"I named her Midnight," Jeff called after her.

Joelle went angrily down to the new barn and stood outside the foal's stall for several minutes. She didn't want to do this. Finally, she took a deep breath and went inside.

The foal shrank back against the wall, hiding behind the brown mare. Blossom ambled slowly over to Joelle and thrust her nose at the girl.

"No treats," Joelle snapped. Instantly, she was flooded with remorse. She couldn't remember when she'd ever snapped at a horse. "I'm sorry, Blossom," she said to the old mare.

The mare turned away, and Joelle stood watching the foal. She waited until the foal took a couple of tentative steps toward her, then she reached out with the halter in her hand. Suspiciously, the foal sniffed, retreated, then stepped bravely forward once again. Her bright eyes took in Joelle's hand and her nostrils worked in and out.

"Oh, stop being difficult," Joelle said.

The foal backed up and hid behind the mare. Joelle walked quietly toward Blossom, but she couldn't get near the foal. It soon became apparent that the filly had no intention of letting her slip the halter over her head. She ducked and retreated behind Blossom every chance she got. Finally, Joelle threw down the halter in disgust and stomped up to the house.

"Well, I tried," she said shortly to her mother before she bolted up to her room.

The same thing happened the next day. And the next. Finally, Joelle decided she'd better change her approach. Taking the halter, she slipped into the paddock outside the new barn and stood perfectly still. The foal hid behind Blossom as always, but soon her curiosity got the better of her. She walked forward a few steps, then a few more, and still Joelle didn't move. Finally, the filly stood in front of her and sniffed the pink halter. Joelle didn't budge. The filly began to investigate Joelle's clothes, and after a while Joelle slowly moved the halter so that it rested in the filly's fuzzy mane. The foal shivered but didn't dart away. Joelle rubbed her with the halter, bringing it slowly under her neck, under her jaw, and over her nose. Then she slowly placed the halter over the foal's head.

Whew, she thought. *Foal handling is a lot of work. That foal book I read made it seem like so much fun. Hah! The people in the book looked happy and the foals looked cute and sweet. Well, I don't feel happy, and this filly is anything but sweet.*

"You know, kiddo," Mrs. Latham said one day, watching Joelle tug on the foal's lead, "Midnight needs love as well as training. It'll make things easier. She won't resist you so much."

Joelle frowned at the foal, who had planted her tiny hooves in the hard-packed dirt. "It wouldn't make any difference. She's just naturally stubborn."

She didn't care what her mother said. She wasn't ever going to love the foal who'd killed her beloved horse. She resumed her prodding.

"Come on, Midnight," Jeff cajoled.

"That's not her name," Joelle snapped. "I haven't named her yet."

"What are you going to name her?" Jeff persisted.

"Nothing for now," she said simply. "I'll call her Foal."

"That's dumb."

Joelle shrugged. Why wouldn't people leave her alone? She was keeping her end of the bargain and handling the foal. That was all she had promised to do.

Seven

FOR SEVERAL DAYS, JOELLE CONTINUED TRYING TO halter-break the foal. Sometimes, she couldn't even manage to get the halter over the foal's head. Occasionally Jeff would insist on coming down and watching her while she worked. When he was there, Joelle would try not to let her impatience show. But she found it hard not to lose her temper when Jeff started making suggestions.

"Midnight doesn't like you to pull on her head that way," he'd say when Joelle tried to muscle the foal into accepting the halter.

One day she told him she didn't want him to come with her when she went to work with the filly.

"I'm not being mean or anything, but your talk distracts her and makes her not listen to me," Joelle explained.

"Fine. I'll just go down by myself," Jeff replied. Joelle knew she had hurt her brother's feelings, but she couldn't bring herself to change her mind.

The days slipped into weeks, and before Joelle knew it, it was May—and still the foal would hardly allow herself to be haltered. Joelle got a sinking feeling in her stomach. A two-month-old foal ought to know more than how to have a halter placed on her. She tried to think back to what her foal book had said about training at this early stage. She couldn't remember. Foals were supposed to sleep a lot, eat a lot, and just grow, Joelle tried to convince herself. They really didn't need to be with people that much yet. They couldn't even be ridden until they were two years old, for goodness' sake.

But her father didn't see it the same way.

"Maybe I'm no foal expert, but I can tell you that by now that filly should be well used to being led, and you should have taught her to stand to be groomed," Mr. Latham grumbled, observing Joelle and the filly battling it out one hot afternoon. "I had assumed that you were working with this filly. Now I see that I'll have to keep a closer eye on you."

Joelle resolved to work harder just so her father would get off her back. And for a few days she stepped up her efforts. She checked out the foal book again, but it didn't say much. It explained halter-breaking and breaking to lead, but it kept emphasizing that trust and patience were important, too. "Just spending time with your foal and building love and trust are the most important elements of training," the book said.

That was no help, Joelle thought with annoyance, slamming the book closed. Who wanted to hang around with a stubborn foal? And anyway, Joelle said to herself, the weather was getting warmer. It was just too hot to go down to the dry, dusty paddock and fight with a foal who didn't want to be taught.

In early June, Joelle started trying to lead the filly. The foal allowed herself to be led around grudgingly once in a while. But more often than not, she'd pull back and have a real contest of wills with Joelle. One afternoon, during a particularly tough session, Laura stopped and leaned on the paddock rail, watching Joelle and the foal stare each other down.

"You know, if you'd just talk to her," Laura offered, "she'd get to know you better and trust you more."

Joelle wiped away the perspiration building up on her forehead and put some slack in the lead rope. "Everyone's always got suggestions for me," she muttered. She looked at Laura's eager face for a moment and got an idea—one that wouldn't hurt the foal any, but would help her. "You know," Joelle began, "maybe I'm just not suited to this foal's personality. Maybe she'd be better off working with you." Seeing Laura's doubtful look, she continued hastily, "I don't mean for a long time. Just for a while—through this period. I've never been around foals before. I don't really know what to do."

Laura narrowed her eyes at Joelle. "You know your parents would murder me if I took over for you. This is your filly, and you're supposed to train her."

Joelle sighed. "But I've got finals next week, and I've been so distracted with my studying that I can't really concentrate on her like I should. And you're so—oh, I don't know—horses respond to you."

Laura appeared to give it some thought. But then she said, "Horses used to respond to you. You used to be Windswept's best rider. I used to lay odds on you that you'd end up riding in the Olympics one day or something." Joelle felt a stab of pride, but then she realized that it wasn't true anymore. Laura had said "used to." That meant when she had Dancer. Her eyes filled with tears and she threw an accusatory glance at the foal.

"Yeah, well, I can't be expected to be a great rider when I don't have a great horse, can I?" she said. "Come on, Laura. Help me out for a while. I'm so sick of this filly."

Laura climbed over the paddock rail and took the lead from Joelle. She shrugged. "Okay. Just for a while. But remember, you can't sit around and just wait to get over Dancer's death. You've got to decide at some point that you're going to take action to recover."

Joelle was startled. She'd never heard Laura talk so much to anyone except a horse. Still, she didn't wait to hear more. She wasn't going to give Laura a chance to change her mind.

She left the paddock without a backward glance and headed toward the barn office. She passed the crossties, where Jeff was just dismounting after a lesson on Bluebell. He was talking and laughing as Mr. Latham lifted him down into his wheelchair.

"You should have seen me, Joelle," he boasted, taking off his helmet and shaking his sweaty head. "I walked over some poles on the ground. I'm going to be jumping soon."

Mr. Latham unbuckled Bluebell's girth and lifted the lightweight saddle off the fat pony's back. "It might be a while before you jump, but you're doing great. He's making so much progress, we don't need sidewalkers anymore," he told Joelle. "His muscles are strong enough to support himself."

"That's great, Jeff," Joelle said. Riding was paying off for her brother in so many ways. He seemed happier lately, more a part of the family. His attitude was improving, too, which meant easier therapy sessions every morning. And that was helping reduce her mother's load.

"Good old pony," Joelle said gratefully to Bluebell. She unbuckled the neck strap her father had put on to provide a handhold for Jeff. Then she picked up a sponge and started wiping away the pony's sweat.

"Carry on, Joelle, will you?" Mr. Latham asked, patting the pony on the rump. "I need to give Ghost a workout. The Silver Spur show is coming up."

"I'm going to go see Midnight," Jeff said, racing away to the paddock.

Joelle shrugged. Let Jeff hang out with the foal. At least she was free of the stubborn creature for a while, thanks to Laura. Things were looking up. Well, except for finals. They were going to be the pits. Joelle knew she was going to have to study like crazy if she was going to pass.

"Okay, so we have killer finals coming up, and we're supposed to fuel our brains on this stuff?" Kendra gestured to the grayish lump on her lunch tray. She was the last to arrive at the noisy lunch table in the middle school's cafeteria. Joelle and Nicole were already there, books open, eating the lunches they had brought from home.

"There is something to be said for home cooking," Nicole said wickedly, taking a huge bite of her chicken sandwich for Kendra's benefit. "You don't have to wait in a cafeteria line, for one thing, and it doesn't look like yesterday's science experiment, for another!"

A couple of the girls around them laughed.

"Shhh!" Joelle said to Nicole irritably. "I'm trying to study, and your comedy routine isn't helping me any."

"Well, pardon us, Ms. Grumpmeister," Nicole replied lightly. She turned to Kendra and the two of them started talking in low voices. Joelle tried to turn her attention back to her book, but every once in a while she could hear bits of her friends' conversation. After a few minutes, they started talking about the Silver Spur horse show, so she tuned out.

"Joelle, Joelle, I'm talking to you," Nicole's voice broke in.

"What?" Joelle said, getting annoyed.

A hurt look flashed across Nicole's face. "Oh, forget it. You're no fun anymore, anyway."

Joelle shoved her books in her backpack and jumped up from the table. If her friends were going to be jerks, she would leave and go to the library, where it didn't matter if she were a laugh a minute or not.

"Joelle! Joelle, stop!" she heard Nicole and Kendra running after her. Sighing, she turned around. "Why should I? I'm just ruining your fun," she shouted.

Nicole and Kendra looked guiltily at each other. "Oh, come on. That's not fair," Kendra began.

"We weren't being mean," Nicole took over. "We just don't understand you anymore. We know Dancer's death was awful for you. But that was months ago. Aren't you ever going to be the old Joelle again? I can't bear to think of this summer if you're not going to hang out with us at the barn and talk horses and stuff."

Joelle felt like crying. She really hadn't been much of a friend to Nicole and Kendra lately. But didn't her feelings count, too? Still, she knew she couldn't stand it if she lost her friends. Losing

Dancer was bad enough. "I'll try harder," she said softly.

And over the next few days, she did just that. She pretended to be interested when Nicole brought over the newest riding catalog to let her see the show clothes she wanted for her birthday. She put the pink halter on the foal for Nicole's benefit, and showed her what it looked like against the foal's black coat.

"She's beautiful," Nicole gasped.

Joelle nodded and pretended she agreed. The truth was, though, that she couldn't see any beauty in the tall, gangly foal. To her, the foal only meant sadness—and a terrible sense of obligation. But she didn't tell her best friend about her deal with Laura.

Laura kept her word and led the foal around in the paddock. If Joelle's parents were anywhere around the barn, Joelle would make a halfhearted show of grooming the filly. The minute she felt she could get away with it, Joelle would take off for the house, pretending she had to study for her finals.

It seemed like the last day of school would never come, but Joelle finally walked out of her last class. She'd at least managed to salvage her math and history grades, but English was another story.

"Hooray! It's summer!" Nicole shouted as they met up at their lockers. She threw her notebook up in the air, and papers spewed into the hallway.

"Nicole!" Joelle was horrified. She glanced around quickly to make sure there weren't any teachers watching.

"Oh, don't worry about that," Nicole said, bending over to gather her papers. "I'm going to pick it all up. It was just symbolic."

Joelle groaned. Their English teacher had talked all semester long about symbolism in literature. "I can't believe I did so badly in English," she moaned. "I should have studied more last week."

"Well, I know you weren't down at the barn much, so what's your excuse?" Nicole said dryly.

"Oh, I had stuff to do," Joelle answered vaguely. *I was thinking,* she said to herself as they dodged other students and headed toward the bus. *About all the plans I had for Dancer this summer.*

"Joelle, you're not listening to me."

"Sorry," Joelle said, trying to return to reality. She wished she didn't have to. It was too depressing.

"No more school. Cool, huh?" Devin called from his locker. "Guess I'll see you at the shows!"

"You, too," Nicole called. "See ya."

Joelle managed a weak smile.

"Joelle, he was trying to be nice. Couldn't you have at least talked to him?" Nicole asked.

Joelle shrugged. "How can you forgive him so easily for all the mean things he did at the horse shows?"

"He hasn't been that bad lately," Nicole pointed out.

"Whatever. But I won't see him at the shows, that's for sure," Joelle said.

The two walked along in silence for a while.

"So you aren't going to go to any shows, huh? Are you going to come down to the barn at all this summer?"

Joelle nodded. "Some. My parents say I have to start trailer-breaking the foal. I'm just not that interested."

Nicole shifted her books and looked away. "Listen, I know it's a sore subject and all, but maybe you ought to give the foal to Jeff," she said. "Every time I'm at the barn, I see him hanging around her. He sings to her and makes up these weird games with her. Besides, you really don't like her."

Joelle gasped. Nicole's comment was like a slap in the face.

"Oh, forget it," Nicole said hastily, seeing Joelle's reaction. "Me and my big mouth again. I didn't mean it. I just don't want you to be sad anymore, and I think the foal reminds you too much of Dancer. Maybe you need another horse so you'll forget about Dancer."

"I don't need another horse to make me forget about Dancer," Joelle said between clenched teeth. "Don't you understand? I don't want to forget about Dancer!"

The girls boarded the bus. Joelle sat down on the hard bus seat and stared out the window. She watched the houses and trees whiz by and wished she could stay on the bus and never have to go home.

"Aw, Joelle, come on down to the barn and watch the lessons for once," Nicole pleaded when the bus dropped them off. "It's so boring without you. Now that summer vacation's here, your dad's going to work really hard with the juniors. He's giving extra lessons to the kids who are going to show a lot. We'll have fun."

Joelle didn't answer.

"Please? Even just to help me?" Nicole pressed. "I want to show those Oak Meadows people. Melanie Hawkins has been bragging to everyone how much better her riding's gotten since she left Windswept and went to Oak Meadows. She says Windswept's not that good. You've got to help me prove her wrong."

Joelle kicked the ground with her toe. Maybe she should ride. It was getting hard to refuse all the people who were pushing her to stay involved with horses. She was tired.

She sighed and nodded. "I'll go get my riding clothes," she mumbled, and headed to the house. She changed into her breeches and boots and went back to the barn.

When she walked into the office, Mrs. Latham looked up from her desk. If she was surprised to see Joelle in her riding clothes, she didn't let it register on her face. She merely glanced at the board.

"You can ride Jupiter today," she said. "Dad's schooling some of the juniors in ring two, if you want to join them for a jumping lesson."

Joelle shrugged and grabbed her dusty velvet hunt cap off a bookshelf.

"By the way, Jeff had a wonderful ride. He's in

your filly's stall celebrating with her."

"Mmmm."

Joelle went into the tack room and grabbed Jupiter's saddle, bridle, and breastplate.

"Lucky," said Nicole when Joelle appeared with Jupiter. "I wish I could ride her today. I still haven't forgiven Valor for tossing me in the dust at the spring horse show. Jerky old Melanie reminds me about it every chance she gets."

"I'd give you Jupiter, but my dad wouldn't let me get away with it," sighed Joelle. She straightened her shoulders. "Still, if you're serious about your riding, you have to stop blaming the horse and figure out where you went wrong."

Nicole laughed so hard she nearly dropped her dandy brush.

"What's so funny?" grumbled Joelle.

"You! I swear, you lecture just like your dad." Nicole regarded her friend closely. "You do still want to be a trainer, don't you?" Joelle picked up her braided reins. It did feel good to be back up on a horse again. "Oh, I don't know," she sighed. "Everything's so weird lately."

The girls headed for the ring and started their warmup walking. After a while, Jupiter began moving freely and easily, so Joelle took up some rein, closed her seat slightly, and made Jupiter gradually collect. She pressed her heels slowly inward and applied some pressure with the inside of her calf muscles to make Jupiter move out at the walk. She grimaced—her legs were stiff and unresponsive. After a few turns around the ring, it was time to break into a trot. Joelle let Jupiter find her rhythm, and gradually asked her to extend her trot. Joelle's calf muscles began to protest at the punishment. She had just made a transition to a collected canter when her father showed up at the ring rail.

"Joelle, you're here!" Mr. Latham made no effort to hide his surprise. He grinned broadly, his white, evenly spaced teeth showing. "Okay, that's it," her father called. "Move those horses forward. I want to see good brisk rising trots."

Joelle's body rose and fell with the familiar diagonals. Up when the outside leg moved forward, down when it came back. Up-down-up-down. She grimaced. Her leg muscles were no longer used to this. As she continued posting, her legs ached from the unaccustomed exercise. Well, she wasn't going to stop so soon. When her father asked the class to slow and collect to a sitting trot, Joelle clenched her teeth and obeyed him. She endured the pain, and was relieved when she could finally let her body relax into the gentle flowing motion of the canter.

"Okay," Mr. Latham said, pointing to a crossrail in front of him. "Pop over this crossrail a couple of times."

Joelle gathered the horse under her and headed toward the small jump. Jupiter was nothing like Dancer, she thought wryly as she rabbit-hopped over the fence. The girls went around each other, taking turns at the fence. Joelle couldn't seem to find her distance with Jupiter. For the first jump she was too late, and the next one caught her too early, nearly unseating her. How embarrassing!

Nicole was also having a hard time. And when they started over a low vertical, it really showed. She leaned forward and applied heavy leg pressure just before Valor took off. Valor gave a little buck after the fence.

"You're riding way too aggressively. You're going to land in the dirt if you keep riding Valor like that," Mr. Latham told Nicole.

Nicole made a face and went to the back of the line. "I can't do anything right."

"Next time," Mr. Latham said. "Let's see you take that one better, Tara," he called to the girl riding Chips.

Tara found her distance right away.

"Perfect!" Mr. Latham said, beaming.

Nicole and Joelle rolled their eyes at each other.

Then it was Nicole's turn again. This time, Mr. Latham gave her a small course to ride: over a vertical, then a right turn to the brush jump, around the corner to the in-and-out, and finishing up with an oxer.

"Wish me luck," she whispered as she started off on the course.

"Go with the bend. Bend him around your leg at the corner. . . . Not bad!" Mr. Latham said when she finished.

Nicole patted Valor's sweaty neck and heaved a sigh of relief.

"Now it's your turn to wish me luck," Joelle whispered as she squeezed her heels into Jupiter's sides. She cantered toward the vertical. Just before the fence, Jupiter put in an extra stride. Joelle, who was leaning too far forward, lurched up on her shoulder.

"Straighten up!" barked her father.

Sitting back upright, Joelle drove with her seat toward the next fence.

"Too defensive. Jupiter never refuses a fence, so why are you muscling her?"

Joelle felt hot tears sting her eyes as she steadied herself for the next fence. Why did her father have to pick on her?

This time Jupiter took off long, and Joelle felt herself become unseated again. She clutched at Jupiter's mane and somehow managed to stay aboard. Nothing was going right! She was crazy to have joined in the jumping lesson!

Mr. Latham shook his head. "Fix it. Relax and steady."

Gritting her teeth, Joelle approached the fence. She was determined. She leaned forward and got up into a two-point position. *One-two-three, one-two-three, find the distance . . . there it is.* Jupiter sailed up over the first jump effortlessly, took one stride, then completed the second jump. Joelle smiled and patted Jupiter's neck on her landing. She cantered toward the group and pulled up to cheers and whoops.

Mr. Latham sighed and smiled, then turned immediately to his next student.

"Wow! That was great!" Nicole said. "You haven't lost your touch."

Joelle beamed, then reached down and patted Jupiter's neck again. It was now dark with sweat, and there were little flecks of foam on her reins. "It felt good," she said.

Suddenly, thoughts of other jumps crossed her mind. Dancer taking her over a huge triple at the Oakdale summer horse show the year before. Dancer taking her over the brick wall at Oak Meadows the year before that. *Oh, Dancer!* Joelle felt the pleasure of her ride fade immediately. She shouldn't have come out to the ring. She urged Jupiter forward, to keep her walking.

"Dad, may I be excused?" she asked thickly after a while.

Her father nodded. "Sure. She's cool enough. Let's quit on a good note," he said. "The rest of you, here's your next course . . ."

Joelle picked up her reins and passed her father. He patted her leg as she rode out the ring gate.

What good note? she thought as she dismounted. *I feel miserable.* She ran up her stirrup irons and loosened Jupiter's girth. Jupiter nudged her. "Oh, it's not your fault, girl. It's me," she said sadly.

She led Jupiter over to the crossties and untacked her. Then she groomed her, using her sponge to wipe away the sweat that had accumulated around

Jupiter's neck and chest area. After a vigorous toweling, she picked out the horse's hooves and dressed them. Finally, she blanketed the chestnut and led her to her stall.

"Joelle, have you worked with your filly today?" Mrs. Latham called as she passed Jupiter's stall. "Laura won't be doing that for you anymore. I just spoke with her. She's got other responsibilities."

Joelle frowned. She hoped that Laura hadn't gotten into trouble because of their arrangement.

"On my way," Joelle replied cheerfully. But as soon as her mother had passed, she made a face. There was no avoiding it. She was on her own with the foal.

As soon as the filly saw Joelle she ran and hid behind her adopted mother. She peeked out from behind Blossom and reached over to bite a fly on her back. The brown mare lifted her head and watched Joelle for a moment, then went back to munching hay.

"Hello, Foal," Joelle said with a sigh. "You hate it as much as I do, but we have to have our lead-line lesson."

She slipped on the pink halter, went outside, and made her familiar rounds of the paddock. Joelle had to stop numerous times to coax the reluctant filly forward. She was really beginning to lose patience when Jeff entered the paddock.

"Hi, Midnight," he called.

"What are you doing here?" Joelle snapped.

"I was gonna ask you the same question," Jeff responded.

"You shouldn't enter a stall or a paddock in your chair," Joelle pointed out. "Mom will be furious. You could get hurt."

"So what?" Jeff thrust his chin out.

Immediately the foal jerked away from Joelle and trotted over to Jeff. She showed no fear of the chair. She shoved her nose into his lap, and Jeff ran his hands over her. He picked up her lead and pressed the control on his chair, moving it forward. The foal walked docilely along beside him.

Joelle put her hands on her hips. "Fine!" she shouted. "Why don't you just take over?"

Jeff stuck his tongue out at his sister. "I already asked Mom if I could have Midnight, and she said no, that she's yours. It's not my fault that she likes me and not you."

Joelle didn't wait to hear any more. She stomped out of the paddock and bolted up to the house.

Eight

THE NEXT DAY, JOELLE FOUND LAURA IN THE FEED ROOM and apologized to her.

Laura shrugged. "Oh, it wasn't a problem. But your mother's right. You're the one who needs to work with the foal. She's got to learn to respond to you."

Joelle continued her work halfheartedly. June turned into July, and still Joelle couldn't see much progress. Often, after her hot, dusty battles with the foal, Joelle would have only enough energy to flop on her bed for the rest of the afternoon. It was beginning to feel like the longest summer of her life.

"I love summer vacation," Jeff said one evening after dinner. "No school. Just riding every day."

Joelle pressed the buttons on the remote control of the TV.

"Turn down the volume, will you?" her father said distractedly. His head was bent over a show premium.

"Any good classes?" Mrs. Latham asked. "Some of my younger riders are clamoring to go to a show."

"The usual. Some hunter classes, some equitation classes. A good class for some of the beginners—equitation over fences for age eleven and under, with two-and-a-half-foot jumps," Mr. Latham replied. "Hey, here's a new one. Wake-up hunters. First thing in the morning. Good idea." He took a pencil off the counter and started scribbling names next to various classes. "Joelle, there are some good classes here for Kendra. Low fences. The other juniors will be able to enter some medal qualifiers. Nicole needs to polish her equitation, so I'm going to enter her in a few of those classes. We've got to get that together by the time the Silver Spur fall show rolls around."

Joelle felt her heart thud into her stomach. This time the year before, she'd had big plans for the Silver Spur fall show. The foal was to have been weaned from Dancer by September, and Joelle would have had a month to get Dancer fine-tuned for the October show. She shook her head to rid herself of the thought and pressed the buttons on the remote again.

"Joelle." Mrs. Latham's voice broke into her thoughts. "What about you? Do you want to ride Soldier at this little schooling show next week?"

111

Joelle shook her head and wished they would leave her alone.

"Why not?" Jeff asked.

Joelle shot him a look and swallowed hard. "Because I don't want to," she answered.

"Why not?" Jeff persisted.

She looked at her parents with pleading eyes.

Mrs. Latham gave in. "Okay, we won't push you. It's just that the little kids look up to you. When you do well in a show, they square their shoulders and realize they can get in that ring, too."

"I can't show without Dancer," Joelle said quietly.

Mr. Latham set down the list and pursed his lips. "Listen, Joelle, we've been through this. It's been several months now, and none of us is ever going to forget Dancer." He paused and looked at the ceiling for a moment. When he spoke, his voice sounded far away. "But there are other horses who need us. There's work to be done, and we're the only ones who can do it."

"If you're mad at me because I'm not helping at the riding school, I'll do more work around the house or something. I can give Jeff his baths and help you with his therapy. I just don't want to be around the barn that much anymore."

"I don't need help with my baths. I do them myself now," Jeff said.

"You don't need to take on more household work," Mrs. Latham cut in quickly. "And we've managed to do without you at the riding school. That's not the point. I want to see you spend more time with that filly of yours. It's breaking my heart to see her so lonely. And the time spent with her now will set the stage for her future training. She's got great bloodlines. She's built well and she's sweet. She deserves a chance."

"At least I spend time with her," Jeff supplied, ignoring Joelle's scowl.

"That helps, Jeff," Mr. Latham cut in. "But the filly needs one person training her who loves her and believes in her. That's what helps horses come to trust humans. All trainers know that this is how you get a star horse to realize its potential."

Joelle blinked back tears. She'd never heard her father sound so disapproving of her. "Oh, I don't know," Joelle said lamely. She stood up and wiped her eyes on her sleeve. "It's just that nothing's the same anymore. The foal is stubborn and I miss Dancer and I'm just mixed up."

"Well, be that as it may," her father continued, "you have a bargain to keep. You agreed to take care of the foal. After she's weaned we can sell her. Maybe someone else will give her the time and attention she deserves."

"No!" wailed Jeff.

"Dave—" Mrs. Latham began.

"I'm serious!" Mr. Latham thundered, and stalked out of the room.

Joelle looked at her feet.

"Look what you've done! I don't want to sell the filly! I love her even if you don't!" Jeff yelled at Joelle. He wheeled his chair out of the room.

"I suppose you're mad at me, too," Joelle said to her mother.

Mrs. Latham sighed. "No, dear. I'm concerned. But it's a difficult situation. Tell you what—let's have a cup of tea." The two of them headed into the kitchen, where Joelle slumped into a chair and eyed her mother.

"Did I ever tell you about when I was a girl and my parents lost our horse farm?" Mrs. Latham asked as she put the teakettle on the stove. She sat down while she waited for the kettle to whistle. "Your grandfather got thrown by a sour jumper named Red Hot, and he was badly hurt. We couldn't keep up the place. We had to move to New York City, and we lived in this horrid little apartment by the railroad yard. My parents were miserable, and so was I."

Joelle sat up and watched her mother pour the steaming tea.

"I thought I'd hate horses forever for what they had done to my family," Mrs. Latham went on. "And I was glad we were in the city, where I didn't ever have to see them. But it didn't last long. Right in the middle of one of the busiest cities in the United States, I found a riding school. The horses were terribly neglected, and I found that I loved horses again. In fact, those horses needed me."

"What does that have to do with me?" Joelle asked.

"The point is, horses have unintentionally hurt you, but your love for them will never go away.

114

That filly needs love and care now. Before long, she's going to be weaned, and she'll need you more and more. If you just shut her away in her stall, she's going to grow up suspicious of humans." Mrs. Latham waited a moment before delivering her final argument. "Dancer wouldn't have wanted that, would she?"

Joelle wiped the tears from her eyes for a few seconds. "No," she finally agreed. "She wouldn't have. But Mom," she confessed, "I can't help it. I don't love her. I hate her for what happened to Dancer."

"Oh, honey," her mother said, getting up to hug Joelle. "The love will come in time. You just have to trust me."

The next morning, Joelle lay in bed for a while and looked around her room. She'd never gotten around to redecorating it, so it was still bleak and bare. But a warm Santa Ana wind was blowing through her open window, and she could hear birds chirping on a branch outside. From down the hill came the sounds of horses banging against their feed bins. If she strained her ears, she could hear the hands calling to each other as they went on their morning feed rounds. There were a few hungry whinnies.

It was a subtle pull, but Joelle found herself responding to it. The warm smells of the barn were beginning to seem more inviting than her boring bedroom. Joelle threw back her covers, jumped in the shower, and dressed in jeans and a sleeveless T-shirt. The day would be hot.

Outside, Joelle waved to Laura, who was in the feed room, and then continued over to C Barn. She passed the creek bed on the way, and was shocked to see how dry it was. There were weeds growing in the parched, cracked dirt. There were even a few tumbleweeds bounding along. Joelle could hardly believe this was the same creek that used to bubble busily, stretching from bank to bank, inviting horses to step in and cool their tired legs after a brisk riding lesson. Joelle closed her eyes and remembered a summer day a couple of years earlier when she and Dancer had decided to follow the creek as far as they could. She'd packed a picnic lunch and—

The sound of a shrill whinny pierced her memory. It was the foal, Joelle knew. With a sigh, she continued on toward the paddock outside the new barn. She stood there for a moment, watching the horses within.

Mare and foal were grazing. Or rather, the foal was grazing in between nipping at an occasional fly and playing chase-my-tail. Joelle couldn't help but laugh at some of her comical antics. Suddenly, the foal darted around, chasing a shadow, then turned and tangled up her legs like a pretzel. She went down in a heap and sat there looking bewildered.

Joelle climbed into the paddock and patted the mare for a while. She couldn't help it if she wasn't Dancer. She'd done the best she could. Joelle looked at the foal and reached out with her fingers, encouraging her to step closer. The foal wheeled away and went back to her games.

Sighing, Joelle left the paddock and went up to the barn office. Out of habit, she took the riding schedule off her mother's desk and filled in the horse and ring assignments on the board. It wasn't long before her parents and Jeff came down and the parking lot started filling up. The day was beginning.

"Oh, there you are," her father said. "Give me a hand getting some horses tacked up. I've got to go grade the ring before my first jumping lesson."

Joelle shrugged and agreed. What else was there to do, anyway?

On the morning of the schooling show, Joelle sat in the kitchen with her mother and Jeff.

"Are you sure you don't want to go? All your friends will be there."

Joelle nodded. "I'm sure, Mom. I don't feel like going. It'll be too hot."

"Well, you're right. It *is* going to be hot. I hope your father is able to find a shady place to park the vans. I can't bear it if the horses are uncomfortable."

"Oh, don't worry, Mom," Jeff said. "Dad always knows what to do."

Mrs. Latham stood up. "Okay. Let's go. Things are quiet at the barn, but I think we'll find plenty to do. We'll turn out some horses, since the paddocks will be free, and organize the tack room. I'll take

117

you around on Bluebell if you'd like, Jeff."

The day passed quickly, and it was dark before the horse vans rumbled up the driveway at Windswept. A few cars followed, filled with young riders and their parents. Joelle ran up to greet everyone as they pulled to a stop by the barns. She could hear the horses knocking around inside. A few whinnied. They were glad to be home after a long, hot day at a show.

Nicole ran up to Joelle waving a handful of ribbons. "Look! Look, Joelle! I qualified for a medal, and won two thirds and a second! Valor was so good today."

Although Joelle was happy for her friend, she felt a knot of disappointment form in her throat. If she'd gone to the show, maybe she would have won a medal, too.

Kendra climbed out after Nicole. "I got two fourths, and a second in a really big hunter class."

"All right!" Joelle exclaimed.

"We haven't told you the best part!" Nicole's eyes were bright.

"Yeah!" breathed Kendra.

"Come on, junior horsepersons," Mr. Latham cut in. "Start helping me unload these campaigners. They've worked hard. They want their stalls and dinner. You can talk as you work."

The girls walked toward the back of the vans.

"Tell me!" Joelle said.

"You see, it's like this—" began Nicole. But she stopped as the first horse was led down the

118

rubber-padded unloading ramp.

"That's Blade Runner!" gasped Joelle. "Devin Butler's horse!"

"And Megaton's right behind him," Nicole burst out. "That's what we wanted to tell you. Devin got in a huge fight with his trainer and said he was going to give up riding. Dr. Butler talked to your father and then your father talked to Devin, and here he is." Nicole paused for air, then continued, "He had the worst day at the show. He kept missing his distances and got excused from one class for having three refusals."

"I'm not surprised," Joelle murmured. "He rides those poor horses so roughly. They were bound to begin stopping sooner or later."

"Melanie Hawkins will be livid that he's moved here. Isn't it cool?" Nicole exclaimed.

"Cool? Who cares?" Joelle didn't want Devin to ride at Windswept. She liked Dr. Butler, but his son was another matter. He was rude, and he used riding to make trouble for other people. She didn't really care for the trainers at Oak Meadows, but still she felt sorry for them because they had to deal with Devin. Devin would probably start quarreling with her father if things didn't go his way. But she knew she'd have to be nice to him. He was now a Windswept customer.

"Quit flapping your gums, girls," Mr. Latham said, thrusting Blade Runner's lead rope into Joelle's hand. "Joelle, this is Devin Butler's horse."

As if she didn't know!

119

"Put him in stall number seven in C Barn. We'll put Megaton next to him."

"This is great," Mrs. Latham said to Joelle, reaching over to adjust the buckle on Blade Runner's blanket. "Dr. Butler talked to me about this a couple of months ago, but I wasn't sure that Devin would be willing to leave Oak Meadows."

"He's only coming here to waste our time," Joelle grumbled.

Her mother pushed back a few stray hairs from Joelle's face. "He's a nice boy. He's just had trouble getting over his sister's death. And anyway, we have a business to run. There's no excuse for giving less than our best to anyone who wants to ride with us. Or for not taking the best care we possibly can of their horses."

Joelle shrugged and patted Blade Runner on the nose. He was a beautiful horse. He couldn't help it if Devin was his owner.

"You'll need to take Blade's shipping boots off and wrap his legs," her father said. "I'll be down there to settle him and Megaton in when I get the others unloaded."

Joelle led Blade Runner to his new home. The minute she unclipped his lead rope, he snorted and paced around the stall. She talked soothingly to the big bay, knowing it was important that he settle in to his new home.

A short while later, Nicole brought in Megaton. Once he was in his stall, she came over to Blade Runner's stall, dragging a milk crate behind her. "I finished unbraiding Valor's mane. I don't know where Devin ended up. He stayed at the show after we left. Will you help me unbraid Blade?"

Joelle nodded. Blade Runner was so tall that she'd need a milk crate to stand on, too.

"Isn't this great? Now we'll really show Oak Meadows. Your parents will make a rider out of Devin yet."

Joelle shrugged. "Yeah. And I have to be nice to him. Oh, well."

"I'll bet the Oak Meadows people are all talking about his turning traitor and coming to Windswept."

Joelle smiled in the semidarkness, thinking of the girls who'd left Windswept to ride at Oak Meadows. She hoped they were upset.

Suddenly, the two girls heard the sound of boots coming down the aisle. It was Devin, still wearing his full riding habit. Even in the dim barn light, Joelle was suddenly struck by the way his blue hunt coat set off his dark hair. She shook her head at her thoughts. She couldn't believe she would notice something like that.

"Hi. I was just coming to do that," he said, watching Joelle and Nicole working on his horse.

Joelle frowned and jerked gently at a braid. Well, he was a customer now. She might as well get on with the business of being nice to him.

"How are you?" she asked politely.

Devin shrugged and shoved his hair back with his hand. He leaned up against the stall bars. "Not

121

so good. You must have heard. But your father has some good ideas on how to get me through this plateau I seem to be stuck on."

"What do you mean?" Nicole asked.

"Oh, I've been in a slump lately. Now my horses won't even go around the dinkiest course without trying to stop," he muttered.

"You need to balance both of your horses," Joelle said impulsively. "You need to ride them with more sensitivity. And are your stirrups even? Have you been unconsciously shifting your weight?"

Devin stared at her for a moment. "I don't know. But it's a thought." He changed the subject. "So where's this filly my father's been telling me so much about?"

Leave it to him to remind me about the foal, Joelle thought. She jerked her head to the right. "At the end. That last stall."

"How's she doing?"

"Oh, fine. I've broken her to lead and she's set to be weaned in a couple of weeks." Joelle tried to sound enthusiastic. It didn't matter what Devin thought, but she didn't want Dr. Butler to find out how she felt about the foal. She had too much respect for the vet.

Devin disappeared down the aisle.

Joelle turned back to Blade Runner's braids. "What does he want to see the foal for? She's just a foal," she whispered to Nicole.

"She is not. She's beautiful," insisted Nicole. "Anyway, maybe he feels weird because his father had to . . . well, you know."

"She looks good," Devin said when he came back. "Nice head. Good slope to her shoulders."

Joelle grunted and finished undoing the last braid. She patted Blade Runner's neck and let herself out of the stall.

"You know," Devin said, "I'm going on vacation with my parents for a couple of weeks."

"That's nice," Joelle said politely.

"I'll need someone to ride my horses." Devin's eyes searched hers.

Joelle looked away. "I'm sure my parents will ride them," she said.

"I know they would. But they're busy. When they can't, will you ride them for me?" Devin asked.

Joelle was startled. He wanted her to ride his horses? "I don't ride much anymore," she said.

He met her eyes. "Please?"

Joelle was shocked. Why her? Still, if it meant that much to Devin . . . "Well, sure. If my parents okay it."

"I already asked your father. I've seen you ride. I know you'll take good care of them." With that, he strode out of the barn.

"Wow!" Nicole burst out.

"Weird," Joelle stated flatly. Had this been arranged by her parents to get her riding again? She put the thought out of her mind and decided that she actually couldn't wait to try out Devin's horses. Would their performance live up to their good conformation? She was too curious to pass on this opportunity to find out.

Two days later, Mr. Latham asked Joelle to tack up Blade Runner. "Let's see what we can do for that horse."

Joelle needed no urging. She saddled and bridled Blade Runner, then led him out to the ring. She climbed aboard, adjusted the girth and her stirrup leathers, then rode into ring two.

"Let's start him out easy," her father said, standing in the middle of the ring. "He needs to get used to the new sights and sounds."

"Okay," Joelle called. She let her reins go long as she started the big bay out on his walk, riding him on the buckle so he'd stretch his head low. "He's so huge," she called to her father. Nothing like dainty Dancer. But he felt good. He moved out with a big rangy stride and looked around curiously.

Joelle adjusted her girth again and then slowly brought in her reins to collect him at the walk. After a few circles, she moved into her routine of trotting and a warmup canter. His canter was a fluid, rocking motion, and Joelle went with it naturally.

"He's some horse," Joelle said admiringly in spite of herself.

Her father frowned. "He's leaning against the bit more than I'd like. Gather him under you some more."

"Easier said than done." But Joelle concentrated and called upon every ounce of her skill to get him to balance up. He'd gotten into the habit of leaning forward. It was hard work getting him to listen to her and shift his weight back to his powerful hindquarters. After a while, Joelle could feel sweat trickling from under her schooling helmet.

"That'll do for today. He needs a break from jumping. But we have some work to do over the next few weeks for the fall show. Cool him down, and I'll go get Megaton. I'll bet Devin's had the same problem with him. It's from hunching forward the way he does. It throws the horse's weight off."

By the end of the day Joelle was tired. But as she headed over to the foal's stall she found herself whistling. It had been fun working with two new horses and analyzing their problems. And there was no doubt about it—they were both high-caliber horses with a lot of potential.

"They were so big and powerful. I can't wait to jump them," she said to the filly conversationally as she led her around just before sunset. She chatted happily to the foal and didn't even realize that the foal was walking along willingly, with no trace of her usual stubbornness.

Nine

DEVIN CAME BACK TWO WEEKS LATER.

"Thanks for taking care of my horses," he said to Joelle.

Joelle regarded him for a moment. There was something different about him. She couldn't quite put her finger on it. Maybe it was his eyes. They didn't look so . . . angry. Maybe his vacation had relaxed him, Joelle decided.

"You're welcome. I enjoyed riding them. They're great horses," she said sincerely.

Devin nodded. "My parents gave them to me. I guess they were hoping that if I started focusing in on horses, I'd start throwing my heart into something besides thinking about Valerie."

Joelle's head jerked up. It was the first time she'd ever heard Devin refer to his sister.

"You still miss her, don't you?" Joelle said.

"Yeah," Devin answered quietly. But he straightened up and turned to his horses.

Joelle thought about Devin and his sister that afternoon as she led the filly around for her lesson.

"I guess Valerie's death is probably why Devin's been such a megajerk," Joelle told the filly as she groomed her later. "It must have been awful. I can see how he'd be sad and angry. But it was so long ago. And his horses took the brunt of his problems. Poor Blade Runner and Megaton."

At first, Joelle missed riding Blade Runner and Megaton. But she hung around and watched Devin's lessons over the next few days and was glad to see that he was making progress. Both of his horses seemed to be balancing themselves more, which helped when it came time to take them over the fences. Devin wasn't hunching over quite as much, either.

And there was more good news. Jeff was starting to work with his braces. He was gradually using his wheelchair less and less, and often could be seen walking haltingly around the barn on his crutches.

"It's his riding," Joelle heard her mother tell their grandmother on the phone one day. "He doesn't know he's having therapy. He just thinks he's having fun."

Mrs. Latham seemed to be right. Jeff was happier and was working harder than ever at his therapy. Joelle decided that as long as Jeff was improving, the summer wasn't entirely a waste.

*   *   *

127

During the dry, hot month of August, she continued breaking the foal to the lead. Mr. Latham insisted that she have the filly spend some time apart from Blossom, so Joelle started taking her on long walks on the trails surrounding the Windswept grounds. At first the foal whinnied anxiously for her stepmother, but each day she got less and less excitable.

One afternoon Joelle led Blossom away and fed the foal in a horse trailer her father had parked in the paddock so she'd get used to the idea of walking in and out of the trailer.

"One thing's for sure, she's not going to give us as much trouble as Ghost does when she's trailered," Mr. Latham said approvingly as he watched the foal walk eagerly up the ramp to her food. "She'll be easy to load up for the horse shows."

Joelle shrugged. "Who cares?"

"Joelle, if you don't stop it, Dad's going to remember what he said about selling her," Jeff said in a low voice, glaring at his sister as their father walked off to his next lesson.

Joelle shoved her hands in her jeans pockets. Although her father hadn't mentioned selling the foal lately, Joelle thought it might be a good idea. She felt guilty about it—after all, Jeff loved her. But Jeff wouldn't be able to train the foal. So what was the point of keeping her?

One afternoon, as she returned from a trail walk with the foal, Devin stopped her.

"Tomorrow I'm taking a day off from schooling.

Your dad's worried the horses will get sour from working so much," he said. "So why don't we pony your filly behind Megaton? Megaton's calm. You can ride him while you lead the filly, and I'll hack Blade Runner. It'll be good for them to go out on the trail."

Joelle was surprised. Devin had been nicer lately, but now it seemed that he was actually going out of his way to help her. He didn't have to worry about her and her problems with the foal. But it would be nice to have company when she was walking with the stubborn filly.

"Joelle's got a date!" Jeff teased her at dinner that evening.

Joelle rolled her eyes. "I'd hardly call walking along with a filly a date."

The next morning after breakfast, she met Devin at the barn. They groomed Blade Runner and Megaton, talking while they worked. Joelle haltered the foal and led her out to the mounting block, and Devin held her while Joelle mounted Megaton. He climbed aboard Blade Runner, and they set off on the trail. Right away, the foal moved along willingly. She seemed to enjoy the company of the two geldings, and she trotted alongside, alert to every sight and sound.

"She's really enjoying this," Devin remarked. "Look at how perky she is."

Joelle turned to watch the filly. She had to admit the young horse did look happy. The foal filled her nostrils with the little breezes blowing by and every so often let out a shrill little neigh.

After they returned to the barn Devin suggested that they get together and pony the foal every few days after his lessons. Joelle agreed. It wasn't so bad spending time with the foal when she could at least ride Megaton and talk with someone. It was easier to forget that the foal was along that way.

"She's going to be a beauty," Devin said one afternoon as they watched her cavort up the trail.

Joelle nodded noncommittally.

"Do you want to stop here and give the horses a rest?" Devin asked at the crest of a small hill overlooking the new barn. They could see the dry creek bed wind like a dusty snake behind Windswept and on toward Horseshoe Dam.

"Okay. They do look pretty hot," Joelle said. She dismounted and sat on a large rock while Devin tied his two horses. The foal gamboled over to her, and Joelle had no choice but to let her nuzzle and search for treats.

"Want some water?" Devin offered Joelle a horn-shaped bota bag he'd tied onto his saddle. After taking a grateful sip, Joelle wiped her mouth and sprinkled some of the cool liquid on her sweaty forehead. Immediately, the foal thrust her nose into Joelle's palm, licking her hand.

"She's thirsty," Devin said. "Give her some water."

Joelle poured water in her palm and cupped it while the filly slurped noisily.

"Take it easy," Joelle laughed.

Devin and Joelle sat in companionable silence for a while, watching the filly's antics. Joelle's attention soon drifted to the view. From her perch on the rock, she had a sweeping vista of the stable area spread out below. If she squinted, she could see her mother in ring one with a group of little kids. In ring two, someone on a gray horse—Soldier?—was having a jumping lesson.

"You know," Devin broke in, "I've really enjoyed riding at Windswept. Your parents are good trainers. I think my riding's improving, and Blade and I don't get into as many battles these days. Your dad's helped a lot."

"Thanks," Joelle said. She was glad that a rider as good as Devin could see and appreciate her parents' skill. And he *had* improved since he'd started riding with them earlier that summer. He was sitting straighter now, thanks to her father's time-honored remedy of having him ride with a riding crop behind his back and locked with his elbows. This was to remind Devin to sit straighter, with his shoulders slightly squared.

"Your dad says I'll be ready for the fall show," Devin continued. "How about you? Are you going to show?"

Joelle looked down at her dusty boots and shifted the lead rope from one hand to another. She shrugged. "I don't think so," she said.

"Why not?"

"I don't know. I guess that ever since I lost

131

Dancer, I just haven't been into horses as much," she confessed.

"A couple of the kids told me that, but since I came here I've seen you help out with the little kids. And you ride my horses and work with your parents' school horses and all. It seems like you're still at least halfway interested," Devin pointed out. "And I see you working with your filly all the time."

Joelle grimaced at the foal, now leaning down and searching the ground for anything resembling a bit of greenery. Her black coat gleamed in the sun, and Joelle was struck by how big she'd grown over the last few weeks.

"I only spend time with her because I have to," she confessed. "It's part of the bargain I made with my parents when they agreed to let me breed Dancer to Trilogy. They didn't want to because they said Windswept was a riding operation, not a breeding operation, and because a foal would be a lot of work." Joelle paused. "I convinced them that I wanted a foal of my very own to train, one out of Dancer. I was dumb enough to believe her foal might be a grand prix jumper." She sighed and looked away, her eyes scanning the hills.

Devin took another sip of water. "You want to ride grand prix jumpers, huh? You know, I used to watch you at the shows on your black horse. You were one of the few girls on the show circuit who were really serious about riding. But you were awfully cool to me."

"You were always causing problems. Remember when you switched the sheets with the courses on them, and Nicole went off course because of it? And then you cut me off on the rail during a big flat class, and I broke stride right in front of the judge."

Devin was quiet for a minute. "Yeah. I was a jerk. I was going through some bad stuff after Valerie died. It was like my parents didn't even notice I was alive, they were so busy missing Valerie. . . . " His voice trailed away. "Anyway, we talked things out. I figured out that I was putting my energy into the wrong places." He shook his head. "I was lucky I wasn't permanently kicked out of the horse shows around here. I don't want to let anything get in the way of my riding again. You know, I want to ride grand prix jumpers one day, too. I also want to ride in shows all over Europe, and—who knows?" He lowered his voice and looked around, like someone might creep up and listen in on his secret. "Maybe even ride on the United States equestrian team in the Olympics."

Joelle was silent for a moment.

"You think I'm crazy, don't you?" Devin's dark eyes watched her intently.

"No," Joelle replied. "You're gutsy. You've got potential. I guess I'm just a little envious. I wish I still had a dream. I just don't want to be involved with horses anymore. Not without Dancer."

Devin stood up and strapped the bota bag back onto his saddle. "My dad has been around horses all his life. He says that it's rare for people to lose

133

their dreams altogether. He says that it's more likely that they misplace them for a while, but if they keep searching, they'll find them again."

Joelle stood up and walked over to untie Megaton. "What else does your dad say, Devin Butler?" she asked teasingly. She was feeling uncomfortable with the intensity of their talk and wanted to lighten the mood.

"He says that being a true horseman isn't about being for one horse," Devin added as he mounted Blade Runner. "He says it's about throwing your heart into horsekind in general."

Joelle felt hot tears prickling the backs of her eyelids. Dr. Butler was a vet. He knew about horses, but what did he know about loving one horse so much that life seemed meaningless without her? But Joelle didn't say anything. Devin would never understand. She sighed and clucked her tongue at the foal, and they walked down the hill toward home.

As August wore on, Joelle found herself pulled more and more into working around the riding school. She wasn't quite sure why. She still didn't feel like riding, but she didn't mind helping the younger kids or giving Devin's horses some exercise. And she spent a lot of time helping Nicole with Valor.

"I don't know how you do it," Joelle's father said one afternoon after Nicole had had a particularly good lesson. He and Joelle were sitting in the barn office between lessons. "Nicole's really concentrating. Maybe she just communicates better with a girl her own age than with a stern old guy like me."

"Oh, Dad," Joelle said, rushing to reassure her father, "she needs your method of training, too. It's just that sometimes she needs to hear things from a friend as well."

Mr. Latham reached over to ruffle his daughter's hair. "Whatever works. But one thing's for sure— you have the makings of a fine trainer. I'm pleased at how you've helped school Devin's horses on their collection and balance. You can already see the improvement they've made over the jumps."

Joelle shrugged. She felt strangely embarrassed discussing Devin with her father, so she changed the subject.

"Where are Mom and Jeff?" she asked. She hadn't seen them since before lunch.

"Jeff had a doctor's appointment, and then they went shopping for back-to-school clothes." Joelle wrinkled up her nose. "Believe me, Mom knew better than to try to drag you clothes shopping," her father said. "She'll do what she usually does— guess at your size, and return whatever doesn't fit."

Joelle let out her breath in relief.

"Anyway, Mom called home after Jeff's appointment and said that his doctor is pleased with his progress. He says Jeff's improvement over the summer has been a miracle. I think our miracle is named Bluebell."

Joelle smiled. "He's like a different kid," she said. "He's happy all the time, and he doesn't whine that much anymore. And he uses his braces more. He's hardly ever in his wheelchair."

"That's so he can spend more time at the barn," her father said. "He likes to be with your filly."

Joelle thought her father was trying to prove something to her. She just mumbled an assent and picked up a show premium to fan herself with. She wasn't going to worry about the foal right then. It was too hot.

Her father interrupted her thoughts. "Will you turn up the air conditioning? I want to cool down a bit before I have to go back to that dusty ring."

Joelle adjusted the knob on the air conditioner, then got two sodas from the refrigerator.

As he sipped his soda Mr. Latham looked out the window at the brown hills. "I hope the Santa Anas don't kick up again this afternoon," he muttered. "I've been worried at how dry the chaparral is this year. That darned drought. We've had too many brush fires lately."

Joelle shivered at the thought of fire racing through their barns. Her overactive imagination could see the horses shrinking back from the flames and—

Her father finished his soda and stood up. "I got the premium for the fall show in the mail today. Guess I'd better get out there and work some of the horses. We don't want Windswept to disgrace itself."

"Oh, Dad, Windswept always does well."

Mr. Latham fired a parting shot over his shoulder. "Maybe. I'd be more confident if you decided to ride at the show." Then he walked off, leaving Joelle to her own confused thoughts. Did she want to show? Of course not. Not without Dancer. But if she didn't, would she really be letting Windswept and her family down?

Squaring her shoulders, she left the office. She had tack to clean, horses to bandage, dirty blankets to pile up for the laundry service. There was no time to think, and Joelle liked it that way.

One afternoon, Jeff accompanied Joelle and the foal on their trail walk. The filly bounded playfully along next to Jeff on his crutches, and she was so docile that Joelle didn't notice how far they'd walked. Finally, she realized that her brother was getting tired, and they turned back toward home.

"I can't believe you're still going," she exclaimed as they approached Windswept's barns.

Jeff nodded. "Yeah. I'm trying to get in shape so I can start school without my wheelchair. Maybe one day I can dump the stupid crutches, too."

Joelle stopped and hugged her brother. "That's the spirit!"

Jeff shrugged. "I guess so." His little sunburned face brightened. "And guess what? Since I'm working so hard, Mom said that I can show Bluebell in the walk-trot class at the fall show."

"Great!"

"You will be there to watch me ride, won't you?"

"Uh . . . yeah, sure." Joelle sighed and pulled more insistently on the lead as the foal balked. She didn't want to go to the fall show. But she definitely didn't want to miss her little brother riding in his very first horse show. He'd worked too hard for this chance.

Before Joelle knew it, the last week of summer vacation had slipped by, and the first day of school was upon them. That morning, Joelle got up early and met Jeff at the breakfast table. Her father was already down at the barn, and her mother was dashing around, packing lunches and making breakfast.

"Today's a big day. Jeff's going back to school without his wheelchair, and your filly's being weaned from Blossom. The mare's owners are coming by this afternoon to take her home," Mrs. Latham said.

"Poor filly. She'll miss Blossom."

"Which is why she'll need her human friends to help her through," Mrs. Latham said, looking pointedly at Joelle. "But it's time. She's six months old."

"Oh," was all Joelle said. She hadn't really thought about weaning. But her mother was right. "I can't believe the foal's already—" she started to say.

"She's a weanling now, so you can't call her 'the foal' anymore," Jeff cut in triumphantly. He picked up his crutches and worked his way over to the counter to grab his lunch. "I guess you'll have to call her something else."

"I'll call her 'the weanling,'" Joelle retorted.

"'The weanling,'" her mother said dryly. "Romantic. Right out of a girls' horse book. What if Anna Sewell had named Black Beauty 'The Weanling' instead?"

Even Joelle smiled. "I'll think of something. But she's just a skinny little foal. She doesn't have a great personality or anything. It's hard to think of a name."

"She's more than a skinny little foal, in case you haven't noticed. It's a wee bit early to tell for sure, but she's got the classic lines of a conformation hunter. Anyway, you've got to look at her more closely. Then naming her will be easier," Mrs. Latham suggested. "Now let's get moving. The school bus will be along any minute."

Joelle hugged her little brother and wished him luck at school. She was glad that he didn't seem nervous.

The first day of eighth grade wasn't too bad. Joelle and her friends had quite a few classes together and even the same lunch period. Unfortunately, all Nicole and Kendra wanted to talk about at lunch was the horse show coming up in a few weeks. Joelle tried to be excited, too. She thought of Jeff's riding in his first show.

"And did you know?" Joelle told her friends excitedly. "Jeff's starting back at school without his wheelchair. He's using his crutches most of the time now. Because of his riding therapy, the doctor thinks he could be walking without crutches by next spring."

"Horse power!" Nicole said with a grin. "The great healer."

Kendra turned to Joelle. "It really is, you know," she said quietly.

Joelle set down her sandwich and sighed. "People don't heal when they lose a horse like Dancer," she informed Kendra. "I'll miss her forever."

"Of course you will," Nicole cut in hastily. "But you can still do other things while you're missing her. Like be excited about your filly. It seems as though you couldn't care less about her."

"I care about her some," Joelle lied. The way Nicole put it, Joelle felt like a jerk. She did feel sorry for the way the filly would feel when Blossom was led away later that day. That proved she cared about her, didn't it? At least it proved she didn't hate her. "By the way, she's being weaned today, so I can't call her 'the foal' anymore."

"What will you call her?" Both of her friends looked at her expectantly.

"The weanling!" Joelle said.

Nicole started to laugh, until she realized that Joelle was serious.

Ten

"HELLO, WEANLING," JOELLE SAID TO THE FILLY WHEN she got to the paddock that afternoon.

Jeff was already there, patting the foal and singing some song in a low voice. "She's all upset," he said, turning to Joelle. "Laura said she's been running all around the paddock since Blossom left. Poor little Midnight."

Joelle leaned against the fence and studied the filly. Her black coat was glistening with sweat and she was obviously agitated. She'd nuzzle Jeff, but every few seconds she'd trot off to circle the paddock, letting out a series of frantic, shrill whinnies.

"The foal book says that weaning is harder on some foals than others," Joelle said, shoving her hands in her pockets.

"I'm going to the tack shop with Mom," Jeff said. "Maybe while I'm there I'll buy Midnight something to cheer her up. They have horse toys, don't they?"

Joelle shrugged. "The filly doesn't need a toy. She just needs time to get used to being without Blossom."

Jeff patted the filly and picked up his crutches. "Do you want to come to the tack shop, too?"

"No, not really," Joelle said. She didn't have anything better to do, but the idea of a trip to the tack shop didn't appeal to her. She turned away from the filly and walked with her brother back to the house.

After her mother and Jeff left, Joelle wandered into the living room and turned on the stereo. She frowned when she heard a public-service announcement reminding people to continue to conserve water. Joelle wondered if the drought would ever end. She changed the station and listened to music until her mother and Jeff got back from the tack shop. Joelle decided to go see what they'd bought.

"I got new jodhpurs and jodhpur boots for the show," Jeff exclaimed, bursting through the door with Mrs. Latham trailing behind.

Joelle studied the cream-colored jodhpurs and rubbed her hand over the leather of the boots. "Nice."

"Look at what else I got!" Jeff pulled a big plastic apple tied to a length of cord out of the bag. "It's a toy apple for Midnight," he announced. "I bought it with my allowance. Now she'll cheer up."

Joelle looked at the apple. "Horses don't play tetherball," she said.

Jeff shook his head at her. "You don't know anything about foals. I'll get Laura to tie it to her stall bars so she can push it around with her nose. Can I go down and show it to Midnight, Mom? I told her I was buying her a surprise, and she's waiting to see it."

Mrs. Latham laughed and let him go.

Joelle saw her mother look at her, but she turned away and went inside to set the table. Why did her brother keep trying to make her look bad in front of her parents? At least now that school had started, there'd be less time for him to hang around the barn, singing and playing silly games with the foal. *Honestly. Sometimes he acts awfully young for his age!* she thought irritably.

"It's only the first week of school. I can't believe how much homework they pile on us," Joelle wailed to Nicole two evenings later. She'd been puzzling over one math problem for at least half an hour. Finally, she'd called Nicole for help. Together, they'd managed to work out the solution.

"Eighth grade is a lot harder than seventh," Nicole complained. "And next week we're going to miss two days of school for the horse show. We'll get so behind."

Joelle didn't answer.

"You're going to the show, aren't you?"

Silence.

"Oh, come on, Joelle, we always go to this show. We get to miss school Thursday and Friday and stay at the Five Horses Inn. You know we've always had a blast! And anyway, you've been helping me with Valor and all, but when I get into that show ring, I just know I'll fall apart if you're not there."

"I'll think about it," Joelle said before she hung up.

After she got off the phone, she closed her math book and stared out her window.

Deciding that she wanted a snack break before she started her science homework, she slipped downstairs. As she entered the kitchen she heard her parents talking in low voices in the living room. She knew she shouldn't eavesdrop, but she couldn't help it.

"I just don't know, Dave," came her mother's voice. "It's been six months since Dancer died, and Joelle hasn't gotten over it. I'm worried about her."

"I know it hasn't been easy," Mr. Latham said. "She doesn't seem to be recovering. Most girls her age would cry for a while, then move on to another horse or something. But I guess Joelle had an extra-special bond with Dancer. Maybe it's just taking her longer to work through her grief."

"Oh, Dave, I don't know how long we can wait. Maybe she just doesn't love horses anymore now that Dancer's gone. Maybe we made a mistake insisting that she keep caring for that filly. The poor little thing can't help what happened to Dancer, but Joelle makes her pay the price every day. It seems so awful."

Joelle's hand flew to her mouth. Was that what her parents thought of her? That she was being mean and making the foal pay for what happened to Dancer? She was a Latham. Never in the history of her family had anyone been awful to a horse. Was she the first?

She quickly got some cookies and milk and slipped back up to her room. But try as she might, she couldn't keep her mind on her homework. She kept thinking about what her parents had said. Was she really that mean to the filly? Finally, she pulled out one of the photos of Dancer she'd ripped off her bulletin board. She studied the picture for a while, letting her eyes move slowly over Dancer's muscular body, taking in her rippling mane and lovely head. She looked into those wise eyes that she missed so much. *Oh, Dancer. I'm not trying to be mean,* she thought, gazing at the photo. *But I can't help what I feel. It would be easier if I loved the foal. Everyone would get off my back. Maybe the problem is that I don't love horses at all anymore.*

Joelle tossed and turned all night. The next day at school, she could hardly keep her mind on her classes. That evening, she decided that she would make a real effort to throw her heart back into horses. She would start by going to the fall show. Maybe she could think clearly if she was away from the foal for three days. She'd be surrounded by horses and she'd feel the thrill of the competition. She'd find out for sure if her love for horses had died with Dancer.

"Good," her father said when Joelle announced that she'd be going to the show. "We need your help. Almost all the juniors are going, and we've got a fair number of horses to look after as well. It's going to be a very busy three days."

"You can watch me win the blue ribbon on Bluebell!" Jeffrey yelled. Joelle smiled. Jeff's excitement was contagious.

Before Joelle knew it, it was Wednesday, and the Windswept team was to leave that evening for the horse show.

The eight students who were going to the show had shown up at the barn that afternoon with all their gear. They had helped Laura and the other hands load the horses and the tack trunks. It would take three hours to get to the show, since the vans had to move so slowly. The Lathams liked to get to shows early on the night before, to give the horses a chance to settle in.

Students from Windswept had shown at this particular show every year. In the past, Joelle had looked forward to it, partly because of the long drive with her friends. They would laugh and sing silly songs and have a great time the whole way there. But this year, since she wasn't sure she even wanted to go, she didn't know if she could handle the long drive.

"My teachers aren't thrilled that I'll be missing two days of school for a horse show," Nicole announced to the group sitting in Mr. Latham's big truck. It was five o'clock, and the horse vans were about to leave. "So I told them that we'd have missed another day if your parents didn't drive us there at night. This way we don't waste a school day traveling."

"My English teacher nearly had a cow," Kendra added. "She looked down her nose at me through those little glasses of hers and said, 'Horse show? You'll be missing my class for a horse show?' Like it was some kind of horrible disease!"

Everyone laughed.

"I'm glad we're missing school," Jeff said. "My teacher gives us too much arithmetic to do."

Devin groaned. "It doesn't get any better in middle school, Jeff. My algebra teacher loaded me up with two weeks' worth of work to make up for missing two days!"

Joelle glanced at Devin. He sure was being nice to her little brother. It was almost weird, having to get used to this new Devin. Weird, but nice. Suddenly, she looked down at her shoes. It would be awful if Devin could guess what she was thinking. She was getting as bad as Nicole and Kendra when it came to thinking about boys.

"Well, I've never liked the way this fall show is scheduled, right in the first month of school," Mrs. Latham said. "But I did have a chat with your principal, and I assured him that all of you would find plenty of time to study at the show between your schooling and your classes. Whenever we get the chance, we'll head back to the motel and put in a good study session."

Everyone groaned, but no one really minded. It was actually kind of fun to study in a motel with the commotion of a horse show swirling all around.

Mr. Latham walked up to the truck door. "Okay. All the horses are loaded up and ready to go. Let's get this convoy moved out. Silver Spur Horse Show, here we come!"

"Look out for Windswept," Nicole yelled as the truck's engine roared to life. "We're coming for our championship."

Joelle glanced at Devin. She wondered if he felt strange. This would be the first time he'd be riding for Windswept Riding Academy. Did he miss his friends at Oak Meadows? His face gave no clue.

Mrs. Latham waited until her husband took off in the first horse van. Laura was driving the second van. Mrs. Latham brought up the rear.

"We're off!" Nicole sang. She leaned over and grabbed Joelle's jacket sleeve. "You're awfully quiet. Aren't you the least bit excited?"

Joelle glanced at her little brother, who was bouncing on the truck seat, saying, "I'm posting, I'm posting!"

"Yeah," she said quietly. "I'm the least bit excited."

Of course, she thought, *I'd be more excited if Dancer were in one of the vans with her head sticking out one side.* Then her thoughts drifted to the filly, who was probably dozing in her lonely stall. Suddenly it occurred to Joelle that the foal probably wouldn't even notice that she was gone!

After a while, lulled by the sounds of the radio, Joelle fell asleep. The vans made their way slowly through the night. A few lonely whinnies pierced Joelle's dreams. Was that Dancer's whinny? Joelle struggled to identify it in her sleep. She dreamed that she was on Dancer's back, riding into the show ring at Oak Meadows. In the next second, Joelle was standing in the mist and Dancer was galloping away from her. "Come back," she cried. She turned and saw that she was left with only a small black foal. The foal was looking at her. Appealing to her. Even in her dream, Joelle turned away.

She felt her mother's hand on her shoulder. "You're dreaming, honey," she said. "Wake up."

Joelle moved around sleepily, shaking her head to clear away the nightmare. She sat up and saw that her stablemates were still asleep. After a few minutes, Joelle fell into a dreamless sleep.

She woke up again as they turned into the gates of Silver Spur Riding Club. All around Joelle, kids were sitting up and rubbing sleepy eyes.

"We're here!" Nicole shouted. Her eyes were shining, and her black curls bounced with excitement. Wearily, Joelle leaned back against the seat and looked out over the eerily lit show grounds.

When the vans stopped, the work began. There were horses to be bedded in portable stalls and tack trunks to be carried to the stalls that would function as tack rooms for the duration of the horse show. Laura set up the feed room, and the hands dragged in bags of alfalfa cubes and hay bales. Joelle and her friends put up stall curtains and hooks. Mr. Latham disappeared inside the horse show office.

"Well, our stalls look great, but you all look beat," Mrs. Latham said, surveying the group of tired, dirty kids standing before her. "Let's get you kids back to the motel so you can get some sleep. Our classes start bright and early."

"I'm ready to fall asleep right here," declared Nicole. She removed a couple of wisps of straw from her hair and wiped a smudge of greasy dirt off her face.

They all piled in the car and headed for the motel.

The first morning of the show dawned windy and cool. Joelle and her mother rose early. Joelle dressed and slipped out the door while Mrs. Latham started rousing the rest of Joelle's friends. Joelle walked over to the show grounds and turned out horses in the ring to work them on the longe line. She could see her father and Devin in the other rings doing the same thing. After a while, Mrs. Latham showed up with Jeff and the rest of the kids, all dressed to the nines in their best show clothes. Mr. Latham set the Windswept team to work right away studying their courses. Soon the first few riders mounted their horses and started schooling for the morning classes.

"Don't guys look great in riding clothes?" breathed Nicole, watching Devin as he mounted Blade Runner for his first class. "And have you seen that new guy from Camelot Stables? Talk about handsome. I think I'm in love. So Devin's all yours now."

"I don't want Devin to be all mine," Joelle muttered. "As long as he rides well, that's all I care about."

"You're nervous, aren't you?" Nicole studied her friend. "Everyone from Oak Meadows will be watching to see if he's improved since he started at Windswept."

Joelle nodded and turned to watch her parents schooling the rest of the riders. "I think my dad's a bit on edge," she confessed. "Look at him, delivering lectures faster than the speed of sound."

Nicole turned her gaze to the other schooling ring. "What's Jeff doing?"

Jeff was hobbling on his crutches back and forth over a ground pole someone had laid in the center of the ring.

"He's pretending he's jumping a course," Joelle said fondly. Looking at her brother walking, though haltingly, Joelle was reminded of part of the reason she'd come to the show.

After a while, Devin's class was announced. He took Blade Runner around, and Joelle studied his performance from the ring rail. He put in an extra stride at the first fence, but after that he got every distance. He sat well in his saddle, and bent his horse around every turn, taking each jump smoothly and rhythmically. Good, but not flawless. Still, Joelle was pleased. With any luck at all,

Devin would come out with one of the top ribbons. And when the judge announced that Devin had taken the red, all of Windswept whooped.

"If only I can do as well," said Nicole as she stopped next to Joelle before her first class.

"You just focus and take it slowly and smoothly," Joelle instructed her, lightly patting Valor on the rump for good luck. She reached over and rubbed some dust off Nicole's boots. "Just catch yourself if you start wanting to speed up. This is a hunter course. The idea is to equitate and ride smoothly. Make it look effortless."

"Did you have to remind me?" groaned Nicole. "I'm so nervous."

"Never mind your nervousness," Joelle lectured her best friend. "You just go out there, ride well, and knock 'em dead."

Nicole must have listened, because she took each jump precisely, finding the perfect distance to each fence. The whole effort looked fluid. Nicole and Valor made a perfect team.

When she came out of the ring, Nicole swung herself down from her saddle, pulled off her hunt cap, and leaped over to wrap Joelle in a bear hug. "Don't ever even think about not being a trainer. You're the best!" she cried.

"Careful," Joelle said. "You'll spook Valor." But inside, she glowed. And when she heard Nicole's number called to receive the blue ribbon in her class, Joelle knew that the victory was hers as well.

The next day, Windswept riders kept adding

ribbons to the dark green stable curtains outside their makeshift tack room. Blues, reds, yellows, and more fluttered in the cool breeze.

"We're ahead of Oak Meadows by bunches of points," Kendra said excitedly. "I think we're going to take the championship."

"I hope so," Joelle exclaimed.

By Sunday afternoon, it was clear that Windswept was going to take the junior division championship. But now there was something else on Joelle's mind: the walk-trot class, for riders six to eight years old. Trying to calm her nerves, Joelle polished Jeff's saddle and bridle while Jeff dressed in his full habit. Soon her little brother appeared with her parents leading Bluebell. Jeff was chattering a mile a minute, his hunt cap bobbing as he walked.

Joelle tacked up the pony. She whispered, "Now, you be a perfect angel out in that ring. I mean it. No mischief, and I'll give you a whole bucket of carrots."

She could swear that the pony winked at her.

Finally Jeff mounted, looking proud in the two-sizes-too-big hunt coat that had once belonged to Joelle.

"I'm so proud of you, whatever happens," Joelle whispered, hugging her little brother, then dusting off his jodhpur boots.

"Hey! I can't breathe!" Jeff protested, pushing her away. Then he gathered up his reins, and he and his mother walked smartly toward the ring.

153

Joelle and her father stood outside the ring, watching as Mrs. Latham stopped at the gate and Jeff went into the ring by himself. Joelle held her breath as she watched her brother move out ahead of the other boys and girls on their ponies.

"Look at that!" Mr. Latham exclaimed. "You'd never know that not long ago he was lying in a hospital bed, practically unable to move."

Joelle looked up at her father and saw him wipe his eyes. She felt a little teary herself.

"Those little riders are all awfully cute," whispered Nicole. "But Jeff looks like he really knows what he's doing."

"He does," Joelle answered. She held her breath as the announcer told the class to trot. She watched Bluebell go forward, and Jeff began to post.

"Rise on the outside diagonal," Joelle breathed to herself. Good, her brother was on the correct diagonal.

"He's a Latham, all right," Joelle's father said to his wife, his eyes not moving from the little figure on Bluebell.

Several of the trainers who knew the Lathams came by and clapped Mr. Latham on the back. Joelle would have given anything to have a picture of her father's face right then.

Finally the winner was announced. "First place in the walk-trot class goes to number one twenty-three, Jeffrey Latham, riding Bluebell."

The people on the rail clapped and whooped. Jeff rode Bluebell proudly out of the ring.

"See my ribbon?" he exclaimed.

"Well done," Mr. Latham said calmly. But Joelle knew that underneath his calm exterior, he was bursting with pride.

Later that evening, Joelle sat in the tack room and listened to the horses munching and settling down for the night. Bluebell had his promised bucket of carrots. Windswept had taken the coveted trophy and championship ribbon. It had been a perfect day. Perfect . . . except that Dancer wasn't there.

Joelle grabbed a stick and drew a horse in the dirt. It had long legs and a comical expression on its face. The foal, of course. Joelle wondered what the little horse was doing. Was she asleep in her stall? Was she wondering where Joelle was and why she hadn't come down to give the horse her lessons?

Suddenly Joelle realized something, although she hardly dared admit it to herself. *I miss her. I wonder how she would have done at this show if she'd been older.*

Eleven

AS SOON AS THE VANS AND THE TRUCK RETURNED TO THE Windswept barns, Jeff maneuvered himself out of the cab and disappeared into C Barn.

"Where's he going?" Nicole asked.

Joelle could see her mother's gaze rest on her. "I think I have an idea," Mrs. Latham said.

Mr. Latham dropped the loading ramps and started backing the horses out. With a great clatter, Great Caesar's Ghost was led down. Laura sprang up to take his lead. Then came Valor. Nicole took his lead rope and led him away. When Jupiter was led down, Mr. Latham handed Joelle her rope.

Joelle led the mare down the barn aisle. Passing by the foal's stall, she looked in. There was Jeff, sitting in the straw, cradling the foal's head in his lap. Her eyes were closed in a blissful expression as Jeff stroked her nose and rubbed her ears.

". . . and I was so scared, Midnight, but I just squeezed Bluebell with my heels and we went in that ring," he was saying. "And you know what? We did it!" He fished out the ribbon from his pocket and presented it to the filly. "Look at that!"

The foal whuffled it appreciatively.

Jeff put his arm around her neck and hugged her. "See? I knew you'd like it! Oh, Midnight, I missed you so much, though."

Joelle drew back, confused by her feelings, and continued down the aisle.

Monday morning, Joelle missed the bus. Her mother drove her to school, and she met up with her friends just before the first bell rang.

"Did you see Melanie Hawkins? I'll bet she's sorry she left Windswept for Oak Meadows. She was positively livid when someone congratulated me on our championship," Kendra was telling the group.

"I loved it," Nicole said, grinning. "Ever since my fall at the spring show, she's been giving me the hardest time, teasing me any chance she could." Nicole turned to Joelle. "Is Jeff still floating in the upper stratosphere over his ribbon?"

Joelle nodded. "Yeah. He slept with it under his pillow last night, and brought it to school today to show everyone."

"Hey, I won't be seeing you at lunch," Kendra suddenly put in. "Mean old Mr. Carstens says that during lunch I have to make up a quiz I missed. He didn't like that I skipped school for the horse show."

"Well, it was worth it," Nicole said. "Don't you think?"

The bell rang just then, and Joelle was relieved. She really didn't want to talk about the horse show anymore. Of course, there had been good moments—Jeff's win and Windswept's championship. But it hadn't solved her problem, as she had hoped. She still wasn't sure if she liked horses anymore. And she was still confused about whether she would be letting down her family if she gave them up. Joelle sighed and headed to class.

When she got home that afternoon, she saw a strange truck in the parking lot. Walking closer, she recognized the Oak Meadows logo. That was odd— why was an Oak Meadows truck at Windswept?

Joelle went down to the barn to investigate. As she passed the office Jeff stormed jerkily out on his crutches. His little face was red and angry.

"What's the matter?" Joelle asked.

"Someone's come here to buy Midnight!" he said accusingly. Joelle noticed that his face was streaked with tears.

Joelle didn't get a chance to say anything before Jeff moved away on his crutches with more speed than Joelle had believed possible. She continued down through the barn. As she neared the foal's stall she could see several people gathered around the door.

Mr. Latham turned to Joelle, his eyes unreadable.

"This is my daughter," he said to a tall, well-dressed blond girl in her teens. "She's been responsible for this filly's early training."

Joelle said hello and looked inside. She could see two men running their hands over the filly. Joelle recognized the head trainer at Oak Meadows.

"So what do you think, Dad?" the girl asked the other man.

"Well, she's good-looking for a filly. Tall. Nice conformation. Trilogy's line, all right. He throws big offspring. She has possibilities."

The trainer nodded.

Joelle's eyes traveled over the foal for a moment. It was plain to see that the foal didn't like the strangers standing near her. But she stood still and merely looked at Joelle with silent helplessness.

Joelle turned away and noticed the girl watching her. The girl's eyes slid coolly over Joelle, then she turned back to the foal.

"Well, we might be able to make something of her one day," the girl said. "I want a Trilogy baby. His picture's been in all the magazines, and my friends would be so jealous."

Joelle's thoughts froze on the word *might.* Hah! The foal might be by Trilogy, but she was out of Dance Away, one of the finest show horses in southern California! *Might?*

The men stepped out of the stall and started down the hall with the girl. "We'll call you and let you know what we decide," she called over her shoulder.

As they left, Joelle turned to her father. "You'd

sell the foal to those people?" she asked incredulously.

Mr. Latham shrugged. "Sure. She's wasted around here if you're not willing to turn her into the champion she's capable of becoming. And I've known Hank Ballard a long time. He's trained a lot of winners for Oak Meadows. He recognizes quality."

With that, her father turned away.

Joelle leaned her head up against the stall bars. The foal looked at her reproachfully.

"So you're mad at me, too," Joelle said sadly. "I don't blame you. But I just can't help the way I feel. Oh, stop looking at me like that."

The filly's eyes seemed to look deep into Joelle's soul. Eyes that were so familiar . . .

But it was Jeff's eyes that she couldn't bear to look into at dinner that night.

The next few weeks blended together in Joelle's mind. The days were getting shorter and shorter, and by late October it was starting to get dark soon after school. Joelle worked dutifully with the foal, but she was glad there wasn't much time. She walked the foal around the grounds and watched her friends having their riding lessons. Then it would be time to mix the foal's special supplements and put her in her stall for the night.

One afternoon Joelle found Jeff at the kitchen table looking through a horse magazine.

"What are you doing?" she asked her little brother.

"Trying to find our picture from the horse show," Jeff answered. "Bluebell and me winning our blue ribbon."

Joelle smiled and shook her head. "That issue won't be out for at least a couple of months. This one is old."

"Oh." Jeff's face fell. "You're right. Here's a picture of you jumping Dancer."

Joelle froze. She didn't want to see it, but her eyes strayed over to the picture. It had been taken at one of the last shows she'd ridden at. Dancer was balanced beautifully over the tall stone wall decorated with colorful flowers. Instantly, Joelle was taken back. She could still feel Dancer's powerful body gathered under her that day, making the huge effort to take the big fence. She could remember drinking in the wind as Dancer galloped around the course. She could remember feeling that never before had a horse and rider been so perfectly balanced. But what struck Joelle most was her own smile. She hadn't felt like smiling like that in a long, long time.

"You coming down to the barn?" Joelle snapped, grabbing the magazine and closing it.

"Yeah. I've got to give Bluebell his carrots, and I want to talk to Midnight," Jeff said.

"What do you two talk about?" Joelle wanted to know as they stepped outside. She stopped to pet the barn dogs, who crowded around her, hungry for attention.

Leaning on his crutches so he could reach down

and pat the dogs, Jeff said, "I tell her everything. I told her about when some mean kids at school teased me about my crutches. She nuzzled me, so I knew she understood how bad I felt."

Joelle nodded. At least there was one good thing about the foal: she made Jeff feel better.

More offers for the filly began coming in. Each time, Joelle would feel relieved. But then she'd think of Jeff and be glad when her father turned down the offers. "I'm not giving this filly away for a song," he'd grumble.

As October turned into November the days got chillier. Joelle and her mother went to the tack shop to buy a foal blanket for the filly. When the store clerk asked how old the foal was, Joelle had to think for a moment. "Eight months," she said, then she told the clerk the filly's measurements. The woman climbed up on a ladder and brought down a sturdy green blanket.

"Your filly's pretty big for an eight-month-old," the clerk said as she put the blanket in a bag for Joelle. "This is waterproof, but with this drought, I guess that won't matter."

"Maybe it will rain this winter," Mrs. Latham said hopefully. "The drought has everyone worried."

When they got home from the tack shop, Joelle mentioned the clerk's comments to her father.

"She *is* big. We measured her around for her blanket," Mr. Latham said. "Now let's see how tall she is." He reached for the measuring stick he always kept in the back of the tack room. "She's big, all right," he crowed. "Almost fourteen hands. And she's not even a year old. If she's got the right temperament, she could make a talented jumper one day. She's got the conformation so far, and she's got the size. I'll bet she weighs close to seven hundred pounds."

Joelle grunted noncommittally. It was then that she noticed her father looking at her in a strange way.

"You really don't like this filly, do you?" he said, his eyes searching hers.

She turned away. It sounded so awful when he put it like that.

"I guess maybe your mother and I were wrong to insist that you care for her and start her training. You're going to hold Dancer's death against her forever," he said harshly.

Joelle didn't answer, but she felt big fat tears squeeze out of her eyes. Her father took the foal's lead rope from her. "In that case, I guess I will call Hank over at Oak Meadows. I think he'd be willing to up his offer. We'd be better off selling her right away. We're not equipped to have a yearling running around this place. And she's not giving you any pleasure, so what's the point?"

"You'd really sell her to Oak Meadows?"

Her father nodded. "They may be our rivals, but their trainers take good care of the horses." Mr. Latham turned and led the foal away.

Joelle listened miserably to the sounds of the

foal's hooves clip-clopping down the aisle. There was no sign of the foal's stubbornness now. She walked alongside Mr. Latham easily, without a hint of the misbehavior she reserved for Joelle.

When Jeff heard that his parents were actively pursuing the sale, he glared at Joelle every chance he got. "You're mean," he accused her more than once over the next few days. "She and Bluebell are my best friends."

"I know. But Jeff, she needs to be trained, and you're too young to train her. She'll go to a better home. You can still see her, because she'll live nearby." Joelle knew her words sounded weak.

"Hey, Joelle, I heard you guys are selling your filly," Devin said, coming up behind her at school the next day.

Joelle turned to him. "Yeah," she said quietly.

Devin's eyes searched hers. "But she's your grand prix jumper. She's your chance."

Joelle shrugged helplessly. "It's all so complicated."

Devin put his hand on her arm for a moment. "You'll figure it out," he said before he walked off down the hallway.

I wish I could figure it out, Joelle thought moodily.

The next few days dragged by without changing Joelle's mood. She thought about what Devin had said. Then she tried to imagine keeping the foal for Jeff's sake. But there was no way he could train the filly, and her parents were too busy with the riding school to give the filly the intensive training she'd need. Joelle would then imagine selling the filly, and she'd go down to the paddock and pretend that the filly was gone to see if it hurt. But she felt nothing. Not even when she heard her father haggling with someone on the phone about the price of the filly.

"Hank drives a tough bargain. I won't give a nice filly like this away for next to nothing. Horse traders!" Mr. Latham said in an exasperated tone after he hung up. He and Joelle were down in the barn office organizing things before they went up to dinner. "Well, let's go blanket the horses. It's going to be another chilly night."

Joelle and her father stepped out of the office and began blanketing. "Say, what do you know?" Mr. Latham said as they left the barn, stopping to look up at the dusky sky. "I do believe I see some rain clouds. Naw. It can't be. We haven't had any serious rain for years."

Joelle craned her neck and peered at the dark gray clouds rolling in. It did look like rain.

And sure enough, when Joelle awoke the next day there was a steady sound of rain outside her window. Joelle wished she could snuggle under her covers and enjoy a lazy morning. But it was Monday, and she had school. Sighing, she got up.

"Yahoo!" Nicole whooped when she got on the bus. "Don't you just love rain? Maybe the drought will end soon. And then this spring we can play in the sprinklers again and give the horses long baths in the wash racks," she said happily.

Even Joelle found that her heart was lighter. It was nice not to have to worry about brush fires anymore.

The rain kept coming. The oldest barn developed a couple of small leaks, and Mr. Latham had to get up on the roof with a bucket of patch to smear over the leaky spots. Several of the horses took exception to the noises on the barn roof and pawed and whinnied restlessly in their stalls.

"I was all for rain," Mrs. Latham said at the end of the week, "but enough is enough. I don't like the looks of it."

Joelle was worried, too. Over the weekend, she helped some of the hands set down sandbags at the low end of the new barn. As she worked, she noticed that the foal was standing outside in the rain, huddled and miserable.

"Go inside your warm stall, silly," Joelle said. She tried to lead the foal inside, but she refused to move.

"Go figure horses," Laura laughed, coming by with more sandbags. "You give them a nice, warm, dry place, and they stay out in the rain just the same."

Monday, when Joelle left for school, the rain had subsided. She breathed a sigh of relief, but as she boarded the bus after school the rain started again.

"I'm worried," Joelle confessed to Nicole. "I don't know how much more rain we can take. It doesn't rain for months, and in the last week and a half, we've had nothing but rain."

Nicole nodded and chewed her lip. "My parents are afraid that we'll be having flash floods pretty soon. Look at it." The two girls watched as the rain pounded fiercely against the bus windows. "I'm not supposed to go to the barn today. My mom told me to go right home."

"You won't be missing anything. We sure can't have any lessons. The rings are like soup," Joelle said. She waved good-bye to her friend when the bus stopped at Windswept and raced up the wet driveway to the back door.

"Anybody home?" she called once she was inside. There was no answer. Joelle figured that everyone must be at the barn feeding and bedding down the horses for the night. She grabbed her rain boots out of her closet and jammed them on her feet. They were a size too small, but they'd have to do. Putting on her old rain slicker, she headed outside.

Down at the barn, Joelle saw that there was a commotion. She could hear shouts and whinnies, and she stepped up her pace. Maybe her parents needed her help. Were there more leaks in one of the barns?

She walked down the aisle of the first barn. The horses were blanketed, and though some were moving about their stalls restlessly, they looked fine. "Mom? Dad?" she called.

As she headed out of the back of the barn she saw Laura coming toward her leading Soldier. Laura's hair was plastered to her face, and her green rain slicker flapped in the wind.

"What's going on?" Joelle called.

Laura jerked her head back and struggled to gather her flappy raingear around her. "Trouble at the new barn. The creek's raging. The water's moved up to the back stalls, and we're clearing the stock out. Your parents are down there moving the horses. Some of the hands took the day off, and we're short-handed. We could use your help."

Joelle set off at a brisk run toward the new barn, slowing down as she got closer. Just then a huge rumble of thunder shook the barn. A sharp crack of lightning lit up the sky, and in the eerie light Joelle could see her father in the aisle with Valor. The great dark horse was rearing and plunging, and her father was struggling to control him. Seeing Joelle, he said briskly, "Go help your mom. Bluebell's terrified, but we've got to get him moved up onto higher ground."

Joelle nodded and wiped the rain out of her face. "Mom!" she cried, scurrying over to Bluebell's stall. Inside the stall, she saw her mother cajoling Bluebell, who'd planted his hooves. Mrs. Latham was clucking and pulling gently but insistently on his lead. Seeing Joelle, he took a couple of steps forward.

"Oh, there you are," her mother breathed. "I think I'll be okay with Bluebell here. We're making progress. Go find Jeff, will you? The last I saw him, he was in the feed room trying to scare up some carrots to tempt Bluebell with. Heaven only knows what's keeping him. And then you two see if you can get your filly haltered. She's probably still out in the paddock. Your father should be back in a couple of minutes to give you a hand."

Joelle nodded and walked toward the feed room. Peeking inside, she saw that it was empty. Frowning, she went back up the aisle, checking in each empty stall along the way. Still no Jeff. Where could he be? She felt a flash of annoyance. The place was in a state of confusion, and her parents had their hands full. Leave it to Jeff to make things an even bigger mess. But she didn't want to worry her mother. She'd find him herself.

Suddenly she had an idea. She went over to the filly's stall. No foal. *Figures*, Joelle thought, *the silly thing is probably outside, getting drenched.* Maybe Jeff was already out in the paddock. Joelle went out into the paddock. Instantly her boots sank in the mud. The paddock was a mess! She strained her eyes, but could see no signs of either the foal or Jeff. Her mother had said that the foal was out here. Joelle dashed back inside to get the foal's halter. It wasn't there.

Fighting to control a rising sense of panic, Joelle tore back into the paddock. "Jeff," she called above the sound of the driving rain. "Where are you?" She put her fingers in her mouth and whistled for the foal. But she heard no returning whinny.

Suddenly she noticed that the creek had broken out of its banks. It was now rushing madly along what had once been the lower part of the paddock, the foal's favorite sunning spot in drier times. But now there was no fence, only jagged broken rail. Half of the fence was gone. The foal must have broken out!

Now the panic rose up freely in Joelle's throat. Where was Jeff? And where was her filly? She rushed toward the creek, her fear driving her onward in spite of the rain hurtling mercilessly at her face. The mud made running difficult, and she looked down to find her footing. What she saw in the mud made her cry out in horror. It was one of Jeff's crutches!

Twelve

JOELLE PICKED UP THE CRUTCH AND STARTED RUNNING blindly alongside the creek. If anything had happened to her little brother—no! She couldn't bear to think about it.

"Jeff," she called again and again. She kept her eyes on the muddy waters rushing past her and ran, stumbling, falling, and getting back up again. She felt as though a crushing weight were pressed against her chest, just as she had on the night Dancer died.

As Joelle passed through the broken fence a thought struck her so hard that she slowed for a few seconds. *Jeff went into the paddock to save the foal and he's probably been swept down the creek along with her. And it's all my fault! I didn't even think of her when I found out that the creek was rising.*

In the midst of her jumbled thoughts, she

thought she heard the shrill sound of a whinny. It sounded like a horse in panic. Then came an unmistakably human cry for help.

Joelle ran faster and faster toward the sound, still tripping over fallen tree branches. Above her, the sky seemed to open up and the rain fell in torrents. Now she was at the edge of Windswept's property line. And then she saw the foal at the edge of the creek. The horse was backing up slowly, her small body straining. Her hooves slipped and she scrambled in the mud. But she kept at it, struggling mightily against an unseen weight.

A moment later Joelle heard Jeff's voice calling feebly, "Come on, girl, you can do it. I can't hold on much longer. Don't stop, Midnight. Come on."

Joelle's brain numbly tried to process what she was seeing. The filly was pulling Jeff out of the creek! She was struggling mightily, backing up slowly, slowly, drawing the small boy out of the water that seemed to be sucking at his body. The foal shuddered with the effort, but she kept pulling. Dancer's daughter was saving Joelle's little brother's life!

Joelle sprang forward toward the filly. She reached the black horse just as Jeff was pulled clear of the rushing water.

"Jeffrey!" she yelled. "Jeffrey?"

Jeff looked at his sister and collapsed, letting go of the lead rope. Joelle rushed over and scooped him up in her arms.

"Jeff, Jeff, are you okay?" She hugged the muddy

172

bundle of clothes and boy in her arms. Soon she heard his teeth chattering. She wiped the mud from his face with her sleeve.

Then she heard some noisy gulps and a hiccup, and Jeff started sobbing. Still, the rain pounded them mercilessly. Joelle stretched her slicker over both of them, trying desperately to keep the rain off Jeff. She remembered that when Jeff had fallen out of the tree her parents had been careful not to move him, for fear of further aggravating his injury. She didn't dare move him now. Joelle hoped that by this time her parents had noticed that she and Jeff hadn't come back. She looked anxiously at his purplish lips. They were starting to regain their color. She rubbed her hands over his to restore some warmth to them. Gradually, Jeff stopped sobbing. He lay still, spent by his ordeal.

"Do you hurt anywhere?" she asked him.

"No. Just c-c-cold," he stammered.

Joelle sat with him a while longer. Finally she said, "If I helped you, do you think you could stand?"

Jeff nodded, and gingerly Joelle helped him to his feet. Together they walked haltingly back toward the barn. Joelle wasn't sure what she was supposed to do, but she knew she'd better get him to her parents in a hurry!

Joelle noticed that the foal was following her placidly, as if she were leading her.

"L-look," Jeff sputtered. "Midnight's following us."

"Shhh, cookie breath," Joelle said soothingly. "I know."

"She saved my life, you know," he went on, his small body shivering against her side.

"I saw."

"No, she really did!" Jeff insisted.

"I know," Joelle repeated more forcefully. "Stay quiet. I'm taking you to Mom and Dad. I saw that Midnight saved your life."

That seemed to appease him, and he leaned against her. Joelle took a few more steps, and then she saw her parents hurrying toward her.

"Mom! Dad! I've got Jeff. He's okay. He's okay."

Her father was at her side in an instant, his strong arms lifting Jeff up.

"Oh, Jeff," Mrs. Latham said, laughing and crying at the same time. "What happened? The minute I turned my back, you were gone."

"I went down to see Midnight, and I couldn't find her in her stall. So I went in the paddock, and she wasn't there. I saw that the fence was broken, so I walked along the creek and there she was." He shivered again.

"Let's get him out of this rain," gasped Mrs. Latham.

As they walked Jeff continued, "There wasn't time to call you, so I whistled to her, but she wouldn't come. Finally, I caught up with her by the creek and haltered her. I thought we'd just go through the fence and up toward the old barn, but I fell into the creek. I was still holding the rope, and Midnight pulled me out." Jeff looked at Joelle. "Joelle saw the whole thing. Midnight saved my life. Right?"

Joelle nodded.

Mr. Latham reached over and patted the wet filly now nuzzling up against him. "Good girl," he said.

"Dave," Mrs. Latham said urgently. "We've got all the horses on higher ground. Everything's secure for now. We'd better get Jeff over to the doctor's. There's no telling what may have happened. He could catch pneumonia."

"No way," Jeff assured her. Now that he was safe in his father's arms, he was feeling pretty sure of himself again. "I'm made of tough stuff."

"Don't I know that," Mr. Latham replied, hugging his son. "Good thing, since you tend to get yourself into mischief."

Joelle caught the end of the wet, muddy lead rope and followed her family up to the barn. She was tired and her feet hurt from the too-small rain boots, but it didn't matter now that her little brother was safe.

She turned to look at the filly. Her head was hanging low and her sides heaving from the exertion.

"I'll get the car started," Mrs. Latham said to her husband. "Then I'll swing down here and pick you up."

Mr. Latham looked over at his daughter sternly. "Joelle, while we're gone, you get this filly up to the front barn and put her in stall three. She needs a bran mash and a rubdown."

Joelle nodded. She and the filly walked slowly to drier land. Just then, Laura came dashing down to meet them.

"Look at that poor baby," exclaimed Laura. "She's drenched and muddy. What happened?"

Joelle explained quickly, leaving nothing out. When she'd finished, Laura looked wonderingly at the foal. "She's a hero," she said quietly.

"Yes, I guess she is," Joelle said in a wobbly voice. Her legs were now starting to shake like jelly.

"Well, I'm calling Dr. Butler. He ought to come out and take a look at her."

While Laura made the call, Joelle grabbed some large terry-cloth towels and burlap sacking from the feed room. Rubbing vigorously, she dried every inch of the foal's black coat.

Laura joined in and continued rubbing when Joelle's arms got tired. Standing back, she looked at the filly admiringly. "Well, she doesn't look any the worse for wear, but I'm glad Dr. Butler is on his way."

Joelle went to the feed room. She mixed water and bran in a bucket. Then she plugged in the electric heating stick and waited for it to warm up. When the stick glowed red, Joelle plunged it into the mixture until the mash was steaming. She unplugged the heating stick, then carried the mash to the foal. The filly nibbled at it daintily, savoring the taste.

"Yummy. You like that, don't you?" Joelle crooned, rubbing her ears. The foal turned and looked at Joelle, her dark, warm eyes glowing with affection. Joelle realized that the filly held no grudges. She didn't care that Joelle had worked with her resentfully. In her own horsey way, she forgave freely.

Joelle stood back, not trusting the tumultuous feelings swirling within her. It was too much. She'd gone from disliking the foal to being in her debt—all within the space of an hour.

Laura soon went off to check on the other horses. Joelle leaned up against the foal's dry coat and continued stroking her while the filly licked the pan for the last of the mash.

"Laura's right," she murmured. "You are a hero. How did you know to save Jeff's life?"

She didn't really have to ask. She knew that Jeff had done what she had failed to do. Jeff had spent time loving the foal and talking with her. He'd taught her to trust humans—just what her father had told her she had to do as the filly's trainer. And the foal had responded when Jeff needed her help.

Joelle burst into tears and sobbed into the filly's coat. She cried because she'd misjudged the filly. She cried for all the time she'd lost. She cried because she missed Dancer. But after a while, she also realized she was crying because she was now getting a second chance to make it up to Dancer— and to the foal.

"What have we here?" Joelle's head snapped up at the sound of Dr. Butler's voice. The vet was coming down the aisle, and Devin was with him.

Joelle hastily scrubbed at her eyes.

The vet and his son stepped inside the stall. Dr. Butler set down his big bag immediately. "I heard that this little lady had quite an adventure today."

Joelle nodded vigorously.

"She's some horse," Devin said, patting the foal. The foal nudged him and searched him for treats.

"If you could have seen her! It was unbelievable! It was like an old Lassie movie or something. Only it was a horse!"

Dr. Butler now ran his hands expertly under the foal's jowls, feeling her glands, running his fingertips over the base of her throat. He peered into her eyes and ears with a little flashlight, then opened her mouth and peered down her throat. His hands ran down her legs. He put his stethoscope up to listen to her chest. Then he took her temperature.

"She seems to be fine," he pronounced after a few minutes. "Of course, we'll keep an eye on her."

"I'm not leaving her side," Joelle declared.

Dr. Butler looked at Joelle, then stroked his chin thoughtfully. "I'm glad to hear you say that," he said quietly.

"All right!" Devin added.

Joelle looked down at her shoes. "I know you must think I was a real jerk," she said in a low voice. "But I couldn't help it. I just—I just couldn't love her. I mean, I lost Dancer and it was because of the foal—" Her voice got thick and she choked a little.

"Stop right there," Dr. Butler cut in. "It was not

178

because of the foal. I've been a vet for over twenty years, and I've seen lots of foals being born. And," he added quietly, "I've seen some horses die." He got a bemused look on his face. "I told you before that I haven't ever seen a foal kill a mare. If a mare dies after giving birth, it's because of Mother Nature. We can control many things when it comes to horses. But there are some things we can't—like hemorrhaging. Like what happened to Dancer. To blame it on a tiny little creature who had nothing to do with it is unfair."

Joelle let the words sink in for a few seconds. "Okay, but if that's true, then maybe it's my fault because I was the one who wanted to breed her."

Dr. Butler shook his head. "I'm not letting you have that one, either. You can decide to breed a mare, but you can't determine whether she'll have a filly or a colt. You can't determine if she'll have an easy pregnancy or not. And you can't determine the outcome. You can only do the best that you can with prenatal care and let nature take its course. Well, nature took its course. And we may not like the outcome, but we couldn't have prevented it."

Joelle stood unhappily regarding the foal for a moment. "It just seems so wrong to love and be happy after someone you loved so much dies," she said softly, the tears welling up again. She turned away, facing the wall so Devin wouldn't see her cry.

"Why does it seem so wrong? Consider this: do we really honor someone's memory—even a horse's memory—by being miserable for the rest of our lives? Aren't there better ways to honor someone you loved?"

Joelle tilted her head up and wiped her eyes with her soggy sleeve. This was something she hadn't thought about before. But the more she thought about it, the more it made sense. She turned around. "Maybe there are other ways to honor Dancer," she said wonderingly.

"Yeah," Devin said. "Like turning her daughter into a winner."

Joelle nodded. Dr. Butler put away his stethoscope and stepped out of the stall. "I'll go check on the other horses, but I'll be back in a little while to see if there are any changes in her breathing or anything."

Joelle glanced at Devin. "I guess we both took our problems out on our horses," she said quietly.

Devin put his arm around her and gave her a hug. Then he stood back and laughed a little awkwardly. "Yeah, maybe. But neither of us will make that mistake again."

"No," said Joelle.

"Listen, I'm going to go see if Dad needs any help. Um . . . next week, if you want, I've got tickets to the grand prix. Do you want to go with me?"

Joelle nodded. "Yeah. I'd like that."

Devin disappeared down the aisle, and Joelle stood as if rooted to the ground. She turned to her foal and a misty image of the filly, fully grown, jumping a grand prix course danced across her consciousness.

This filly was Dancer's daughter, tall and elegant, loyal and proud, just like her dam. And a horse as special as this had to have a name. What was it Jeff called her?

"Your name is Midnight," she whispered to her filly, forgotten no more. "And your show name is Midnight Dancer. And before we're through, you're going to hear it many times over the loudspeakers at horse shows all over the United States. Maybe Europe, too. Would you like to be a grand prix jumper?"

The foal nuzzled her and breathed hot little puffs of breath into her ear.

"Oh, Midnight," Joelle said. "We've got so much work to do, you and I!"

created by Joanna Campbell

Read all the books in the Thoroughbred series and experience the thrill of riding and racing, along with Ashleigh Griffen, Samantha McLean, Cindy McLean, and their beloved horses.